DEATH AT MISTRAM MANOR

A 1940s Chief Inspector Bryce story

Peter Zander-Howell

Copyright © 2022 Peter Zander-Howell

All rights reserved

The characters and events portrayed in this book are fictitious. Any similarity to real persons, living or dead, is coincidental and not intended by the author.

No part of this book may be reproduced, or stored in a retrieval system, or transmitted in any form or by any means, electronic, mechanical, photocopying, recording, or otherwise, without express written permission of the publisher.

INTRODUCTION

A funeral service in Oxfordshire has been held for the late chatelaine of Mistram Manor.

The subsequent wake is disrupted by a further death.

Suspicions are aroused, and Scotland Yard is called upon to investigate.

DCI Philip Bryce takes charge, supported by DS Haig and DC Kittow.

PREFACE

Philip Bryce is an unusual policeman. A Cambridge-educated barrister, he joined the Metropolitan Police in 1937 under Lord Trenchard's accelerated promotion scheme. After distinguished army service in WW2, by 1949 he has become Scotland Yard's youngest Detective Chief Inspector.

Bryce's first fiancée was killed during a bombing raid in 1943, and he recently married Veronica, a war widow whom he met during a case.

He is a very private individual, never talking of himself and wary of making close friendships. He is something of a polymath, with a remarkable fund of general knowledge – he has a habit of passing on snippets of that knowledge to people working with him.

CHAPTER 1

The late fifteenth century church of St Anselm, its separate Norman tower standing alongside, lent its beautiful structure and surroundings most fittingly to the afternoon's ceremony. Inside, the carved rood screen divided the chancel – where Beth Hardwicke's nearest relations sat – from the nave, where the remaining mourners sat. The church was small, and the screen, unlike some in larger places of worship, scarcely obstructed the view towards the altar at all.

The final blessing given, the congregants lowered their heads as the late lady of the manor was borne back down the aisle. Pew by pew, they made their way out of the crowded little church and processed behind the family. In subdued pairs and small groups they filed through the neatly kept graveyard, many glancing up at the sky as they went. Several carried umbrellas in anticipation of rain, but for the moment it remained dry.

The principal mourners: Colonel Hardwicke, his son Miles and daughter Esther, together with their spouses and his four grandchildren, assembled first beside the open grave. Hardwicke's two Labrador retrievers, Zena and Zara, well-behaved as always, had waited patiently in the porch during the service, exactly as they always did for Matins on Sundays. Now, they took up station a pace behind their master.

The sexton had dug the grave the previous evening, applying meticulous care to the task. He knew that Hardwicke always required everything to be 'just so'; and if dissatisfied or annoyed in any way, was apt to speak his mind with punishing frankness. The sexton had no wish to antagonise the old man at any time – and especially not while he was burying his wife.

The other sixty or so mourners who had squeezed into the church now arranged themselves in no particular order behind the family. Behind them, spaced all around the numerous yews in the churchyard, were at least fifty more local people who had come to pay their last respects to 'Mrs Beth'. Quite a few eyes were brimful with tears.

The Reverend Simeon Watson conducted the burial service with his usual sympathetic efficiency. His last 'Amen' given, he bowed his head and paused for a moment. Then, raising his voice so it could be clearly heard by all, he announced:

"These solemn rites are now complete. It is Colonel Hardwicke's wish that everyone present, whether in the church party or not, is welcome

– indeed encouraged – to make their way to the manor for the wake. Arrangements have also been made for Miss Dent to bring the children from the school, so that they may join in as well."

An appreciative murmur ran around the churchyard as the unexpected invitation was issued. Few had ever been inside the manor, and for those who had it was always via one of the wing entrances – never through the front door.

The colonel and his family led the way along the path between the church and house. As the mourners set off behind them, it seemed that, almost automatically, social rank was largely restored. The exception to this was the rector. Despite his status as a cadet member of a 'county' family, and a distant relation of the late Beth Hardwicke, he took up the rear of the procession, accompanying an elderly parishioner.

The beautifully proportioned Mistram Manor was now coming into view. Built with local limestone in the Palladian style, it dated from the early eighteenth century. An older house had stood on the spot long before that, built by the same Lord of the Manor who had erected the church. Given the existence of the Norman tower (and the Norman door incorporated into the church itself), it seemed likely that an even earlier manorial property had occupied the site since the eleventh century. Whatever its precise history may have been, Hardwickes had lived at Mistram for over two hundred years – ever since the daughter, and sole heir to the builder of the current house, had married one.

The present squire, Colonel Albert Hardwicke, had been born in the manor in 1880. Like most of his male ancestors, he became a soldier, and had seen a few months of fighting at the end of the second Boer War. But in peacetime promotion was slow. By 1906 he had reached the rank of captain and, were it not for the Great War, would probably have retired, no more than a major, by 1925.

Events in 1914, however, precipitated three promotions in three years and took him to full colonel. After which, serious wounds at the Third Battle of Ypres in the autumn of 1917 saw him invalided out of the service. 'Passchendaele' was a word he never wished to hear again; or even see in print.

On release from hospital, he assumed the running of the estate from his father, inheriting everything when his father died suddenly a year later. Death duties, even allowing for agricultural land concessions, had been substantial. In theory, Lloyd George's 1910 'Acceptance in Lieu' scheme would have allowed the government to accept some land instead of tax, but for various reasons this arrangement didn't work for Mistram Manor. Despite the estate being in good shape, the colonel had still found it necessary to sell several parcels of land and a few art works – all at a time when the market was not ideal.

Thirty years later, and now only a few months from his seventieth birthday, Hardwicke worried that centuries of continuity would cease when he himself died. His son was making a lucrative career at the Bar and had made clear he had no wish to take on the family estate. His daughter, married to an exceptionally prosperous peer who owned sizeable tranches of London and Bristol, had no need of money, and also had no desire to run the estate. He foresaw that he would be the last Hardwicke to own Mistram.

The colonel was pondering this as he walked back to the house, flanked by his son and daughter. Behind were their spouses, each hand-in-hand with a pair of his grandchildren. The big black dogs were now roughly level with the children, one on either side. They trotted along, zigzagging occasionally in a manner similar to escort destroyers accompanying the troop-carrying Queens across the Atlantic during the war. Here, however, the central figures of the cortege maintained their straight course as they approached the broad flight of stone steps leading up to the house.

The indoor staff had returned after the church service. As the family started to ascend, the huge front door was opened by someone who could only be the butler. This was Feeke. Some fifty years of age; of moderate height but overly-moderate width; impeccable in every aspect of appearance, speech, and manner.

"Ah, Feeke, good man," said Hardwicke in greeting. "Has Mrs Walters got everything ready for the influx of guests? I estimate over a hundred will actually come and join us."

"Everything is well in hand, sir," replied the butler, his voice the perfect rumbling depth to suit his stature. "The kitchen staff have done a marvellous job with the victuals. I am confident that no one will go short.

"Mrs Walters thought it would be too difficult for the maids to go around with trays of food; partly because of the nature of some of the items, and partly because our maids are not experienced in that sort of service.

"The food – all cold, of course – is therefore laid out in the dining room, and duplicated in the breakfast room. Mrs Walters thought guests could take their plates and beverages into the parlour, or here into the hall where, as you see, sir, we have assembled additional chairs and tables. Family and close friends are to have the withdrawing room – unless they wish to mix, of course. I've posted a maid or footman at the door of each room to explain to the visitors."

"Excellent, Feeke. I'll apologise later to Mrs Walters and Cook for leaving them to make all these decisions, but my wife..." the colonel stopped, not wishing to finish his sentence in the only way that it could be finished. Instead, he looked towards the open door and relegated his sorrows for the moment with a brusque:

"Now, visitors are piling up the driveway; stand by the door and see them all in – and there's no question of your needing to announce anyone this afternoon, Feeke."

Hardwicke turned to his close family:

"Best if we all split up to begin with, if you don't mind. Miles – I'd like you to act as host in the dining room."

To his daughter-in-law, Angela, he said, "The breakfast room and parlour for you, my dear. The interconnecting doors between the two rooms are to be left fully open today, so the two will be manageable."

To his daughter and her husband, he said:

"Esther and Henry, if would you go to the drawing room and look after our closer friends and the relations who gather in there, I shall stay here in the hall until everyone is inside the house. Then I'll start to circulate." The colonel looked fondly at his grandchildren and said "And you young rabble-rousers – you're free to roam around as you wish."

The adults set off as suggested, while the four youngest members of family turned immediately towards the rooms with the food, hunger pangs making them temporarily forget the loss of their dear Jamjar.

Zara and Zena, who had seated themselves beside their master on entering the house, now turned and padded off towards the kitchen, where they knew how to push open the double-hinged baize door and could be sure of a bowl of water in the scullery.

The colonel positioned himself by the central table in the hall. The exuberant gilding of the table was hidden for the occasion by heavy black stuff, the fabric pooling onto the floor. Framed photographs of his late wife were arranged in an outward-facing circle around an enormous hemisphere of arum lilies. Hardwicke adjusted his black tie and straightened up to his six feet. He felt stale and very tired. Nevertheless, he set his lips into a rictus of a semi-smile, inhaled deeply, and readied himself to do his duty.

Leading the first group of guests were owners of stately houses in the county and beyond, plus a few more who, although lacking land or a mansion, still ranked as 'gentry'. Neither Hardwicke nor his late wife had any surviving older relations, but Beth's sister and her husband, together with a handful of cousins, were among the first arrivals.

The colonel greeted each with a kiss or handshake as appropriate, and then directed them to the breakfast room and dining room.

A number of Beth's friends led the next wave, followed by professional people. Doctor Ford, the aged local GP, arrived with Travis McKay and James Dauntsey, respectively Hardwicke's solicitor and land agent. Next, came several men in their sixties and seventies, each of whom had 'retired army officer' written on him, despite being in civilian clothes. Bringing up the rear came a sprinkling of people in their thirties, childhood friends of his son and daughter, all of whom had known Beth for many years.

As with the first guests, Hardwicke greeted each by name, accepted the continuous stream of condolences automatically, and sent them on to the refreshment rooms. He hadn't been counting, but guessed that more than half the anticipated number had now arrived. Glancing past Feeke and through the front door, he could see the remaining people were hanging back, all apparently unwilling to be first to enter the manor. He strode towards the door and took a couple of paces outside to stand on the threshold. Addressing everyone in a ringing voice he said:

"Come along now, ladies and gentlemen! You are my neighbours and most welcome here. I'm very grateful for your support. Refreshments are waiting for all of you and there is no formality today. My staff will assist you."

He stepped back inside as the villagers trickled forwards. Hardwicke knew the names of his tenant farmers and their wives, and of his own outside staff. However, anticipating that there would be a few names that he either didn't know, or had forgotten, he greeted everyone in this cohort with a firm and friendly handshake.

The last arrival was the buxom village shopkeeper and sub-postmistress, Adelaide

Wilkin. For her, one of his favourite locals, he managed to crack a full smile, and they exchanged a few words beyond those of condolence and acknowledgement.

Hardwicke's eldest grandchild suddenly appeared by his side bearing a plate. Two small triangular sandwiches and a sausage roll were seriously proffered as she said:

"You must eat something, Grandpa."

"Which kind person suggested that to you, m'dear?" he asked, giving Helen a hug as he took the plate.

"It was Graunty. And Gruncle agreed with her."

As the child moved away the colonel was left to work out that it was his sister-in-law Louisa, and her husband Matthew, who had prompted the refreshments – the two being Great Aunt and Great Uncle to his grandchildren.

Hardwicke thought again what an unusual knack his granddaughter had for creating new words. It was Helen who had noticed that her young cousin, Ben, determined to speak but incapable of sounding out the word 'Grandma' correctly, was becoming frustrated by his failures. It was she who had styled Beth 'Jamjar', pointing out that 'jam jar' was what Ben was actually managing to say, and adding that since jam jars were filled with sweetness – "as are you, Grandma" – it seemed an ideal soubriquet.

The memory of how Beth had laughed and

been charmed by her new name, as well as touched by Helen's practical thoughtfulness for her (then toddler) cousin, now came back to the colonel. His wife had asked that the family should all use Jamjar – and to keep using it – even after Ben had learned to master 'Grandma'.

Feeling the unwelcome sting of tears accumulating and a lump building in his throat, Hardwicke was glad to turn his attention to his plate. He quickly made a start on the sandwiches, realising that he was actually very hungry, having skipped both breakfast and lunch. He had had no appetite at the time, and was also not in the mood for either chatter, or depressed silence, over the table.

Feeke, who had temporarily abandoned his post during the lull after Adelaide Wilkin's arrival, now returned to the colonel:

"Everything is running very smoothly, sir. Plates are being well-filled, and the food supplies still look ample."

"Good," replied Hardwicke, "although that may change quite quickly, as I see the school children are hoving into view. I imagine they'll be perpetually famished like my grandchildren." He moved forward to greet the school visitors at the door himself, noticing that the sky was getting darker by the minute.

Led by their energetic young teacher, Vera Dent, a crocodile of sixteen children, the eldest holding hands with the youngest, made their way up the steps. Miss Dent, her golden hair gleaming despite the absence of sun to burnish her halo, halted beside Hardwicke. She expressed her sympathy beautifully, her deep blue eyes full of sincere concern. Shaking the colonel's hand, she added:

"The children and I thank you for your invitation, colonel, and I should like to reassure you that every child has clean hands, and has been instructed on how to behave."

Hardwicke, who had appointed Miss Dent to her post two years before and was very pleased with her performance, told her where to take her charges to find the food, adding:

"I suggest you bring the nippers back into the hall to eat, Vera. There's still plenty of space for all of you to sit together."

Most of the children, aged between five and eleven, looked overawed as they entered the cavernous reception area. Each little girl gave him a quick curtsey as she passed, and each little boy dipped his head.

Hardwicke could now see the rector, walking slowly alongside old Mrs Penny. Before they reached the door, Isla, his younger granddaughter, appeared, bearing a glass of red wine. Unless she had started off with the glass less than half full, it seemed she must have spilt much of the contents on the way. Unknowingly copying her cousin's words, she told her grandfather:

"People are saying you must have something

to drink, Grandpa."

Just as before, Hardwicke accepted the refreshment with a hug for its bearer, jokingly remarking that the butler would have presented the glass on a silver salver, and that Isla would have to borrow one if she wanted to "out-Feeke, Feeke." The little girl giggled, and the butler quietly laughed with her.

As his granddaughter scampered off, Hardwicke immediately drained what remained of the wine. Handing the glass to the butler, he asked for another, "Full this time, please – and you can forget the salver!"

At last, the rector arrived with his elderly parishioner and Hardwicke greeted them both with extra warmth, greatly relieved that this part of his ordeal was almost over.

"A very nice service, rector, thank you. And thank you for coming, Mrs Penny. I'll get Plant to drive you home later; save you another trek. Just say the word when you're ready. Now, do go along and help yourselves to food and drink."

Unlike Miss Dent, Simeon Watson did not always conform to the colonel's preferences. In the twelve years since his arrival the two men had engaged in several animated disagreements, mostly about ritual. These had never caused any long-lasting ill-feeling between them, and in fact the rector was a regular – if not frequent – guest at Hardwicke's table, where liturgical topics were strictly off-limits.

As Hardwicke turned away from the door, Feeke returned with the wine and a more substantial helping of sandwiches and small savouries for his master.

Hardwicke again accepted these gratefully. Attaching himself to the nearest group in the hall he said, "I hope you will all excuse my chewing for the moment, rather than joining in the conversation."

Some of his guests were only too glad of this, not being used to close-range conversation with him at all, and certainly not on any topic that was not work-related.

His plate and glass both cleared, the colonel began to circulate in earnest. Moving every five minutes or so, he made the same small talk as he went from group to group.

He found Vera Dent in a corner of the hall as he had suggested, her charges sitting cross-legged in a semi-circle in front of her. He was pleased that someone had thought to bring cushions from the orangery for his youngest guests. Arriving just quickly enough to stop them all leaping to their feet on his approach, the colonel changed his repertoire for the children. He told them a few facts about the history of the big house, and mentioned that the church and its separate Norman tower were similar to those in a Suffolk village called Bramfield. In parting, he told them to help themselves to all the food and lemonade they liked.

Leaving the hall, he took the corridor towards the breakfast room and stood in the doorway. He saw a dozen or so people gathered in here. Through the interconnecting doors he could see another fifteen or so in the adjoining parlour.

Two of his old army colleagues, concentrating on refilling their glasses, stood at a table by the door. Major General Rossiter, seeing his host arrive empty-handed, immediately poured a third glass of wine:

"Forgive my acting as though you're a guest in your own home, Hardwicke. I know of old that you prefer red, so get that down you."

Lieutenant General Sir Nathan Vickery – fast approaching eighty but still pikestaff straight – passed over a clean plate, telling him:

"And grab some more sustenance while the going is good. Your grandchildren eat heartily enough, but the other kids will no doubt be back in a minute, and a more ravenous flock of little gannets I've never seen."

The colonel collected some bits and pieces and returned to chat with his old colleagues for a while, before moving along to talk to Angela's group, all standing by the interconnecting doors.

"Very well done, Mrs Jeff," Hardwicke told the cook. "Everything is absolutely excellent."

Cook blushed. She was a spare little lady in her fifties who lived on her nerves. Consequently, and rather incongruously given her high level of culinary skill, she looked as though she never sat down to a decent meal herself.

"I'm sure me and the kitchen staff just produced the quantities Mrs Walters said to, sir. I thought it was far too much, but it seems she was right and I was wrong!"

"Be that as it may, you must still take the credit for the quality of the food, Mrs Jeff. I know that we are better fixed than most, because the Home Farm supplies so many of our needs so well. But given the shortages, rationing, and so on, I think even the rector would agree that you have managed your own version of a loaves and fishes miracle today. I thank you very much for that as well."

Cook blushed even more deeply, touched by the colonel's genuine understanding of her efforts. All at once, the accumulated strains of supervising every aspect of the food preparation at short notice, fell away. She suddenly felt herself relaxing for the first time in days, and decided to allow herself another small sherry.

Hardwicke went through to the parlour and immediately spotted the rector (now minus Mrs Penny) in the far corner. Standing a head taller than any other member of this disparate group, Simeon Watson was the central figure gathered by the largest table. He joined them and spoke first to Bixby, a gardener, and his new fiancée Doreen, one of the housemaids.

"My warmest congratulations on your engagement," he said. "You must be sure to give me good notice of your wedding, so that Mr Dauntsey can arrange a suitable cottage for you on the estate."

The couple had hoped for this eventuality, and Hardwicke was pleased with their delighted response. Being a firm believer in the old army officers' mantra of *'feed the horses before the men, and the men before yourself,'* he was diligent in seeing that his staff were all well-treated. At the same time, he was a competent businessman. It was common knowledge that the lure of towns and cities, with their alternative occupations and superior amenities, continued to deplete rural populations after the war. Good staff were hard to find; the colonel didn't want to lose Bixby and Doreen.

Next, he spent some time with Silas Anderson, a tenant farmer, who was standing with his land agent, Dauntsey, and John Edwards, another of Beth's distant relations who was also a cleric like Watson. Small talk completed, Hardwicke left this group with an apology to Dauntsey for being distracted of late, and a promise to make an urgent appointment to discuss work.

Excusing himself as he moved a foot or so past the rector, the colonel repositioned himself beside Marcus Eccles, landlord of the Dog and Partridge inn, and McKay, his solicitor, both standing with Major Hicks, another retired army officer who had been Hardwicke's contemporary at

Sandhurst and so had known him longer than any other person present.

To McKay, Hardwicke confirmed the instruction he had given on the telephone the previous day – that he did not want a 'reading' of the will today. Noting that both Edwards and Dauntsey appeared surprised at this deviation from tradition, the colonel said:

"Completely pointless exercise. No secrets, anyway. Beth wasn't particularly rich in her own right, and apart from token gifts to the grandchildren, there are few bequests – all of them nominal. I am the residual legatee, and McKay and I are joint executors."

Nobody listening showed any sign of disappointment at learning that he or she was not going to be a significant beneficiary. Hardwicke excused himself to speak briefly to Mrs Eccles and Adelaide Wilkin who were sitting by the window, before turning back to the breakfast room.

The two generals, still standing by the breakfast room door, had opted to stay away from the more genteel company in the drawing room, partly to be closer to the wine supply. As the colonel passed them again both men, widowers themselves, gave him understanding smiles and "Bear up, old boy. Soon be over," words of encouragement.

Crossing the hall to the drawing room, Hardwicke was pleased to see that Helen and her five-year-old brother Felix had attached themselves to Miss Dent and her charges, where one of the boys was emptying his pockets of marbles to show them. Old Mrs Penny had also seated herself by the friendly young school teacher and was chattering happily.

Entering the drawing room, the colonel saw at least thirty people were present, some sitting and some standing, yet the room was so large as not to seem crowded, or even well-filled. He steeled himself, and then rapped on a nearby table with a spoon.

"Relations and friends, once again many thanks for coming today. All of you have been in this room before, on happier occasions. But I know that Beth would want you to celebrate her life this afternoon without, as far as possible, sadness and tears. Now, the food levels are probably falling rapidly – my grandchildren have been leading the efforts to eat everything up. So please go and fill your plates again before it's too late. Your glasses too, although be assured we won't run out of drink!"

After some twenty minutes, he returned to the hall, where Miss Dent immediately approached to thank him again for the invitation, telling him that she was ready to take her children away, adding:

"Mrs Penny says that you very kindly offered to have her driven home, colonel, and she is also ready to go."

"Thank you, Vera – I'll organise the car for

her," replied Hardwicke. "Do you want me to make an announcement to the parents that they can take their children now?"

"No, it's all arranged. I've already handed over some children – the remainder can either walk home from the school or, in a few cases, I'll be passing their houses on the way back."

Hardwicke, seeing his chauffeur across the hall, beckoned to him and gave the instruction to bring the car to the front of the house.

It seemed the children and Mrs Penny leaving was a signal for a minor exodus from the manor. Guests began to give him their best wishes and farewells. The colonel was shaking hands with Amos White, another of his gardeners, when a cry came from somewhere in the house.

CHAPTER 2

Hardwicke gave no indication that he was in any way concerned. Instead, he discreetly signalled to Feeke to go and see what had happened while he himself continued to oversee the departures.

Minutes passed before the butler returned and smoothly separated his master from his guests, quietly informing him:

"It's the rector, sir. He has been taken ill in the parlour. Dr Ford is in attendance, and an ambulance has been summoned." Feeke repeated the list of possible afflictions which the old GP had suggested.

"Oh Lord. What an unfortunate ending to an already sad day, Feeke. Tell Mr Miles and Lady Ainscough that I should like to speak to them, please."

His son and daughter quickly joined him, and Hardwicke explained what had happened.

Leaving Miles and Esther as his proxies, Hardwicke hurried along to the parlour to ensure that the rector was as comfortable as possible. Approaching the breakfast room, the colonel felt the first stirrings of a deeper concern. He saw that the two generals were standing in positions that could only be described as 'on guard' outside the now closed door. The parlour door, only a few yards away, was also under their purview – although in fact it was temporarily blocked by a table inside the room.

"We've evicted all the superfluous guests from both rooms, Hardwicke, and I can tell you he looks very bad; very bad indeed," said Vickery bluntly. "As for that quack of yours, Ford, he gives me no confidence. None at all."

Rossiter was quick to agree, "He's blathering about a ragbag of conditions, with appendicitis the front runner. But as a non-medical man who has seen a few cases over the years, I have to say that I don't believe a word of it! Frankly, we've all seen army sawbones in the Boer War who showed more clinical acumen than your man. Never like to cast aspersions, old chap, but you know my motto – if something needs saying, it must be said!"

Rossiter proceeded to offer his own diagnosis, "I think the padre's eaten something nasty. Very nasty. Good job your daughter-in-law was quick off the mark. Made her own assessment and shot off to telephone for an ambulance whilst Ford was dithering."

Hardwicke, who was under no illusions about the elderly medic, made no comment. Had the appointment of the local GP been within his gift, or sphere of influence, (as the appointment of Vera Dent had been,) he felt he would never have chosen Ford. But private medical practices were freely bought and sold. He had always assumed that Ford had simply been the highest – or perhaps the only – bidder for the practice.

The colonel thanked his old colleagues, and went through the breakfast room and into the parlour. The rector was lying on the floor, quite still and apparently unconscious. Someone had brought a cushion for his head; a blanket had also been found and was pulled over the stricken man. Dr Ford, his medical bag retrieved from his car, was sitting by the patient, empty syringe in hand. Angela, kneeling on the floor beside the rector, was now the only other person in the room.

Ford looked up as Hardwicke came in.

"I've given him a strong sedative which seems to have put him out very nicely," the GP reported. "The pain was unbearable; he was going to do himself a mischief kicking and writhing about. Can't say for sure what the trouble might be – appendix is most likely, or maybe a volvulus. Never heard that he is epileptic, but if so it could be a *grand mal* attack. Keen gardener, I hear, so might be tetanus. If it's any of those, hospital is where he needs to be."

Hardwicke looked at the unconscious man's face for a few moments. "Of course," he agreed. "Angie my dear, thank you for calling an ambulance, but this really isn't your problem – I'll get Mrs Walters to take over and see to anything Dr Ford wants."

Angela ran her somewhat stubby fingers through her abundant brown wavy hair and shook her head. "No, it's quite all right, Albert. I'm happy to stay until the ambulance arrives."

"As you wish then; thank you." Hardwicke looked again at the priest on the floor, mentally reviewed what the doctor had said, and then considered Rossiter's alternative suggestion. He made a decision, but kept it to himself for the moment.

The three conscious people carried on an intermittent conversation until two stretcher-bearing ambulance men arrived. A brief discussion between the men and Dr Ford took place, "I have my car here," the GP told them, "I'll follow you to the hospital and see what they have to say."

The rector was loaded onto the stretcher and efficiently whisked away. Snapping his medical bag shut, Ford gave his 'goodbye' to Hardwicke and Angela, and promised to pass on any information from the hospital.

As the patient was being removed, Hardwicke could see that his military friends had disappeared from outside the breakfast room. He closed the door after the doctor, and raised his heavy grey eyebrows at Angela, "Any thoughts, my dear?"

His daughter-in-law, like his son, was a barrister, and also rapidly gathering many professional admirers in legal circles. Only a few weeks before she had been appointed Junior Treasury Counsel, and would soon be prosecuting for the Crown in a serious fraud case. The first two female KCs had been appointed earlier in the year, and Hardwicke had heard on the grapevine that bets were now being laid around the Inns of Court as to whether Miles or Angela would take silk first.

Hardwicke sometimes allowed himself the pleasure of reflecting that in ten or fifteen years it was pretty certain that Miles would either receive a knighthood in his own right, or get one on appointment to the High Court bench. Then both his children, and their spouses, would have a 'handle'. Of course, if women were ever appointed as High Court judges, it was even possible that his daughter-in-law might follow that path to a personal title – rather than a courtesy one – herself.

Angela, her alert hazel eyes a pair of shining windows to a remarkable brain, was to the point in her answer:

"I didn't like the look of him at all, Albert," she said. "There was an awful lot of agonised flailing about. From what I've heard, it doesn't seem like appendicitis. It does look like a stomach problem, though, and I wondered if he'd had a severe reaction to something he ate."

Hardwicke nodded. "Possibly. But between

you and me, I think it may be rather more sinister than a simple food poisoning. I'm going to lock both doors now, and leave everything undisturbed until we learn what the trouble really is. I'll inform the staff – give them some spurious reason for not coming in here. No point in causing alarm, so I'll ask you not to say anything yet, not even to Miles, until the remaining guests have gone. Then we'll have a family chat."

There had never been a key to the interconnecting doors, but both corridor doors had keys. First shutting the connecting doors, the colonel returned to the corridor and turned the breakfast room key in its lock. Without much thought he decided he would do the same for the parlour door – even though a large table had been temporarily brought into that room and positioned in a way which blocked the door. He securely pocketed both keys.

Back in the hall, Hardwicke found that very few people remained. Leaving Miles and Esther to complete the formalities with the last of the leavers, he moved off to the drawing room. A few guests were still gathered in here. Without actually ordering people out of the house, he managed to firmly convey the idea that the wake was over.

It took another fifteen minutes for the last guests to leave. A number had arrived by train, and Plant – after returning from taking Mrs Penny home – made two trips to the station. Other lifts had been given by car-owning locals.

Hardwicke called Feeke and Mrs Walters together and informed them that the breakfast room and parlour were both locked and that no staff should enter either room for the time being, just in case something there had caused food poisoning.

"Mrs Jeff must be told not to worry," he emphasised. "I don't for one moment believe anything she has prepared would be responsible. Please reassure her that sealing the rooms is merely a precaution to isolate the remains of the commercially produced potted meats and fish."

Joining his family in the drawing room, he was glad to see that all four grandchildren were absent, and correctly assumed that someone had arranged for them to go and play elsewhere.

"Well," he began, taking a seat, "I fear there may be a problem. Strictly within these four walls, I don't think Ford has a clue. He listed various, and completely different possibilities for Watson's collapse. Not having any medical training, I can't say that one of them might not be correct. But, from the symptoms which have been described, I have serious doubts about all of Ford's notions.

"We'll have to wait and see, of course, and in the meantime hope for the best. However, I strongly suspect that this is a case of poisoning and, as much it astonishes me to say this, I think it may not be accidental. Anyway, I've sealed the rooms off for the time being."

He looked around at his family. Angela backed him up:

"I agree, Albert," she said. "Simeon wasn't just in pain. He was thrashing around in agony, and even foaming at the mouth a little. I don't think there is much doubt that it was something he ate or drank."

There was a silence as those who had not been near the breakfast room absorbed the new information. Miles articulated the thoughts which others, particularly his father and sister who knew the rector best, had in their minds:

"What you're suggesting, Father, is that Simeon may have been poisoned deliberately. I've heard, and it's probably true, that he's managed to get on the wrong side of a few people, but it's very hard to believe that anyone who didn't get along with him particularly well would go so far as to murder him."

"I agree, Miles, and I'm one of those who doesn't always see eye to eye with Watson myself," replied the colonel. "He's certainly ruffled more than a few feathers in the parish. But that said, he's dedicated and competent. And I'm hardly one to criticise someone who speaks his mind and stands by his principles!

"Anyway, although it will upset Mrs Jeff no end if it turns out he is suffering from food poisoning, it'll be a sight more unpleasant if it's something more sinister. At the moment I don't want to think along those lines. Let's leave the subject until we hear what they say at the hospital."

Standing up to underscore that the conversation had ended, the colonel asked "Who feels like a walk?"

Miles and Henry both pleaded an urgent need to read some work papers, but Esther and Angela were happy to accompany him, and offered to round up the children so that they could also get some exercise and fresh air. Opening the drawing room door, the two retrievers entered, almost as if they had heard the word 'walk'

Minutes later, the little party set off towards the largest of the three lakes on the estate. This was always a scenic and enjoyable excursion, made more so after the short but heavy shower which had released the invigorating smells of washed woodland and loam. The children and dogs gambolled along boisterously, Hardwicke pre-empting any reproof from their mothers by remarking that it was good that the youngsters could let off steam after the sadness of the day.

CHAPTER 3

Back at the manor, Miles was using his father's study whilst Henry worked at the desk in his bedroom. Several maids and one of the footmen were busy clearing away in the hall and dining room, and as soon as the family left the drawing room they moved to clear in there. Restoring order in these areas of the house was not a huge task; many guests had returned their plates and glasses to the dining room before leaving. It wasn't long before Feeke made his inspection and confirmed that he was satisfied, telling all the staff they could now take a break.

Half an hour later, the stillness in the house was broken by the pealing of the front doorbell. The butler, relaxing in the snug privacy of his pantry, quickly shrugged on his jacket and buttoned his waistcoat. Passing through the servant's hall, he waved down both rising footmen, saying, "Sit tight. I'll see to this."

Opening the front door, he was surprised to

see the local police sergeant, Fred Jarvis.

"Good evening, Mr Feeke," Jarvis greeted him courteously, hurrying straight on to explain. "Formal call, I regret to say, as no doubt you're wondering why I'm at the front door."

"You must come in then, sergeant," replied the butler. Eying the sky as he spoke, Feeke saw that dusk was descending and added "The colonel is out in the grounds somewhere, but I expect him back quite soon now."

Jarvis stepped into the hall and stood awkwardly to one side of the door, immediately removing his helmet at the sight of the remembrance table.

Closing the door, Feeke also felt awkward. The circumstances were most unusual, and he was unhappy. Had the policeman arrived at the back door, he would have taken him into the servants' hall, or perhaps into his own pantry. A conventional visitor at the front door would be shown into the parlour to wait there, but that room was now locked. In any case, Feeke wasn't sure if a police sergeant, even on official business, would rank as a conventional visitor.

Before he was obliged to make a decision, he saw Henry coming down the stairs and took the opportunity to obtain advice.

"This is Sergeant Jarvis, here on official business," he announced. "I've told him the colonel is out, and..." Feeke's rumbling voice first paused, and then almost wobbled, as he was forced to admit "...I am unclear as to protocol, m'lord."

"All right Feeke, I'll take the sergeant into the library *pro tem*. See if you can find Mr Miles, and ask him to join us. And keep an eye open for when the colonel gets back."

Turning to Jarvis he introduced himself: "I'm Henry Ainscough, Colonel Hardwicke's son-in-law. Do come along with me, please."

In the library, the police officer was invited to take a seat at a large table.

"This has obviously been a long and sad day for the colonel; can I help you at all, sergeant?" enquired Henry, as he sat down. "Or must you wait for him to return?"

Before Jarvis had a chance to reply, the door opened again, and Miles Hardwicke appeared. He had known the sergeant since childhood, and they shook hands.

Jarvis stammered out some condolence for the loss of Miles' mother, and mentioned that he had attended the service but, being on duty, had been unable to come to the house. He then rushed on with his news:

"I was about to tell his lordship, sir, that Mr Watson passed away. In the ambulance, before it even left the estate."

Jarvis gave his last remark as a statement of fact, not mentioning it was actually an assumption on his part, made simply because his cottage had a view of the estate gates. Returning home earlier, he had observed the ambulance turning onto the road towards the hospital – in absolutely no hurry, and without its bell ringing.

Neither Miles nor Henry betrayed what they were thinking on hearing the sergeant's news. They waited to see what further information was coming – both realising that notification would hardly have been brought to Mistram by a policeman if the cause of death had been one of Dr Ford's guesses.

The sergeant immediately confirmed the worst. "Sorry to have to say, gentlemen, that the rector was poisoned. With strychnine, it seems. I'm here to keep guard on the place where he died, although no doubt everything has been cleaned up since he was taken away. Detectives will be here to take over in due course."

"Poor Simeon," said Miles. "But I'm pleased to say you're wrong on one point, sergeant. Nothing has been cleared away. My father was rather concerned about the rector's symptoms, and after the ambulance came he locked up the parlour and the adjoining breakfast room. I believe absolutely nothing has been touched. However, I can't let you in, as father has the keys with him."

Miles and Henry were thinking along parallel lines. Neither knew the timescale for strychnine poisoning to take effect, although they thought it was fairly rapid. If so, it seemed that the rector must have ingested it whilst in the house. That meant a fair number of suspects, and a very difficult investigation for whoever was in charge –

especially given that many of the guests were now scattered around the county, with a few travelling even further afield.

Before any conversation on the matter could take place, Hardwicke entered the room, having been advised of Jarvis's presence when the walking party returned. The colonel also knew Jarvis well, and greeted him warmly, albeit anticipating what he was about to be told. Jarvis repeated his condolences, and Miles took on the job of explaining the situation to his father.

"This is awful news. Poor Watson," said Hardwicke. "Well, Jarvis, I can't say I'm over-surprised. Whatever Doctor Ford thought might be the trouble, I have to say the symptoms sounded like poisoning to me. Although that impression was only based on the accounts of others, because I didn't see him until he was already unconscious.

"Anyway, as Miles has told you, the breakfast room and the parlour are both locked, and all the windows are closed and can't be opened from the outside. Nothing in the rooms has been touched. I have the keys here, if you want to go in now?"

"Ah.., well..., hmm...," Jarvis prevaricated, the thumb of his right hand wedged under his chin as his index finger rubbed the length of his fine long nose.

"Now there, colonel, you've fairly put me on the back foot, as I'm not sure what's for the best. It's possible that the CID Inspector will come tonight, but on the other hand I know he's very busy thirty miles away."

A little more nose rubbing preceded a sensible prediction followed by a sensible suggestion:

"I believe I may not be guessing too wildly if I say that the Chief will call in the Yard on something this serious. And as you've preserved the room, perhaps it's better if nobody goes in there now – including me – until the big cheese arrives."

Jarvis nodded his head, completely satisfied that he had arrived at the best solution, when an afterthought occurred to him:

"But I'll take the keys, sir, if I might?"

Hardwicke handed over the keys, and enquired what the policeman intended to do next.

"I think I'm to stay here until relieved, whenever that might be. I'll use your telephone, sir, if you don't mind, and tell the Superintendent about the locked rooms. He can give me further orders then."

"Very well, Jarvis. Use the telephone in the hall to contact the station. By all means telephone your wife, too, if you are to be here for some time. I'll get Feeke to look after you – feed you and so on. If you have to stay all night, and if you're allowed to put your feet up and close your eyes, I suggest you use the Chesterfield in the corridor; it's only a few feet from the parlour door. Can you think of anything else for the moment?"

"Only the one thing, sir. The inspector, or whoever takes charge, will no doubt be asking for a list of your guests. Perhaps you could be writing that up in readiness? And would I be correct in thinking that apart from the locals, some of the guests will be miles away by now?"

"A few, yes, but most were more local, or at least from within the county. I'll certainly prepare a list, but I must tell you there were no formal invitations issued, so to some extent memory must serve. My children and I contacted most of the family and closest friends by telephone.

"I spotted you in the churchyard, sergeant, so you'll know that the invitation to the locals was only made there and then, although I'd previously told my staff what was intended. Anyway, I'll consult with Miles and Henry here, and their spouses and children, and between the nine of us we should produce a pretty accurate list. Feeke and the staff will also know quite a few of the guests, so we'll get them involved too."

"Thank you, sir, that sounds ideal. I'm sorry again that this has occurred on top of your own loss."

Hardwicke rose and rang the bell. Feeke appeared, and Hardwicke apprised him of events and issued instructions for the sergeant's comfortable stay.

Having settled the sergeant into his new post and shown him to the telephone, Feeke returned a while later to report that the case had indeed been handed over to Scotland Yard. Jarvis had been told to remain in the house overnight, as the London detectives would not arrive until the next morning.

CHAPTER 4

In a terraced house in Greenford, Alex Haig was sitting contentedly with his wife. He was half-listening to the Light Programme on the wireless as he read – for the third time – a lengthy report in the newspaper spread out before him.

The main topic on the front page of the evening edition was the Old Bailey trial of *'The Marylebone Public Baths Murderer'*. The report was a panegyric for *'Detective Chief Inspector Philip Bryce and his Detective Sergeant, Alexander Haig.'*

Spanning several columns, details were recorded of the evidence presented to the court *'...with intelligent precision by the two police officers...'*

The unfortunate defence counsel, however, was meted a caustic, half-column drubbing, and branded *'...woefully out of his depth when cross-examining the Yard's finest.'*

The report concluded with a rousingly rhetorical: *'Who amongst us is not indebted to men such as Bryce and Haig for assiduously bringing to justice the criminal element in our midst?'*

Fiona Haig was sitting opposite her husband at the chenille-covered table, light from the single bulb in the room nicely illuminating both his newspaper and her complicated Arran knitting pattern. Clothes rationing had ended a few months earlier, and she was enjoying the feel of new wool between her fingers. Looking up, she smiled as she observed how engrossed her husband was, and the obvious pleasure the report gave him. Putting down her pins, she folded her arms, inclined her head to one side, and teasingly remarked in her broad Scots accent:

"I'm no' sure the photographer captured your best side at all there, hinny." With mischievous emphasis and a small sigh, she added, "The chief inspector looks *very* bonny, though. I expect *his* wife will be pleased."

Alex Haig looked up, his dark brown eyes questioning and worried. He had actually been delighted with his photograph. True, when pictured alongside his chief he was neither as tall nor as good looking. But probably few men were, and he nevertheless felt the photograph on the front page was a fair and pleasing likeness.

Fiona's chortle gave away her playfulness and he laughed with her. "Am I getting a wee bit self-absorbed here, then?" he asked.

"Not at all! I'm as pleased and proud as you are – I must ha'e read the whole thing at least three times mysel' before you came home." With which she leaned across the table to plant a kiss on her husband's lips, at the same time admitting "And I think you look *very* bonny in your photograph too!"

The couple settled back to knitting and reading. Their daughter had been tucked up in bed an hour earlier, and they were making the most of their rest when the telephone in the hall rang loudly. Both immediately assumed this would be police-related. Calls were rare, as none of their family – and very few acquaintances – had telephones. Theirs had been installed at the instigation of the Metropolitan Police, when Haig had been promoted to sergeant. Since its arrival, it had rung only three times.

Haig went into the small hallway and lifted the receiver, hoping that the instrument's strident jangles hadn't woken Rosie. The caller was, as he guessed it would be, his boss and fellow *'assiduous bringer to justice of the criminal element'* DCI Philip Bryce.

"Good evening, Alex. Sorry to disturb you, but we've just been handed another murder case – Oxfordshire this time. I'm at home myself, and it's too late to make a start tonight, but I need to outline some arrangements to you this evening.

"Don't come into the city in the morning. Your house is on the way, so I'll pick up the murder bag and a car from the Yard early tomorrow morning. I'll collect you at seven fifteen.

"I have very few details as yet, other than the victim is a clergyman, apparently poisoned during a wake in a local mansion. You should allow for another three-day absence at least, Alex, but be warned that the list of people present is extensive, so it may take a lot longer."

"Aye; that's all crystal clear, guv. I'll be ready and waiting at seven fifteen."

Haig replaced the receiver. Satisfied that there was no sound from upstairs to indicate that Rosie had been disturbed, he returned to break the news to Fiona. She had heard her husband's side of the conversation, and was happy that he didn't have to leave immediately. They could still have their evening and supper together, after which she would pack her his bag.

With the receiver at his end replaced, Bryce thought about his new case. It seemed likely to require a lot of spadework, and he knew from experience that the quality of local officers provided to assist could vary considerably.

He decided to expand his two-man team from the outset, rather than risk having to call for help later, with all the associated waste of time explaining things to a new man. There were three detective constables at the Yard who had impressed him recently, and he plumped for Kittow. Unfortunately, he wasn't on the telephone, but as the DCI had his address he was able to send a telegram. Bryce hoped that the knock on the door wouldn't cause alarm, given that many unexpected telegrams carried only bad news. He dialled the operator and dictated the following:

'Kittow stop Be at Yard 0630 stop Bring bag for minimum three nights away stop Confirm receipt stop Reply paid stop Bryce'

He returned to join his wife in their lounge. This room – like the rest of the house – still needed full furnishing. To that end, Veronica was visiting the auction rooms. She was also slowly gathering choice pieces from the many fine country houses which were being emptied and then demolished to reduce death duties, as the land on which they once stood was then assessed at a lower valuation for tax purposes. In the meantime, the couple were happy to manage with the contents from Bryce's much smaller bachelor flat.

"Another 'first' in our married life, darling," smiled Veronica, referencing the fact that her husband had not been called away to an overnight case since they returned from honeymoon two months before. "Shall I pack a bag for you?"

Bryce plumped down onto the settee beside her and put an arm around her.

"No need, Vee; I have it all organised. The bag at the bottom of my wardrobe is always packed with all the essentials. I'll just add a few clean shirts in the morning."

The couple snuggled up again, to be disturbed an hour later by the telephone. This time it was the operator who dictated:

'Understood sir stop Kittow'

****

The DCI was up well before his colleagues the next morning. He had the greatest distance to travel – from the Brentham Garden Suburb to Scotland Yard – and then out again to Haig's home in Greenford. The journey to the Yard was at least quick, the roads being quiet in the early morning.

He had considered whether to go in from the fairly new Hanger Lane station, a journey which involved a change from the Central Line to the Circle Line at Notting Hill Gate. Or, alternatively, drive in and leave his car at the Yard. But Veronica, ignoring his protests, had insisted on rising early and accompanying him into Westminster, parting from him with a tender kiss, and then driving the Triumph Roadster back home.

In his office, Bryce first attended to an urgent memo which had arrived on his desk overnight, and left a note about it for his secretary. Satisfied that everything else could wait until he returned, he collected Haig's 'murder bag' and made his way back down to the front desk.

He found Kittow waiting a little nervously, small suitcase in hand. Greetings exchanged, the two officers went out to the police Wolseley that Bryce habitually used.

"We're picking up Sergeant Haig," the DCI explained to his young colleague as they loaded their cases into the boot and settled themselves into the vehicle. "I'll drive this morning, but we'll share the load over the course of the investigation, so you'll get a turn soon enough."

"We're going to a place called Mistram Manor," said Bryce as he steered the big car. "When we've collected Haig, I'll tell you both what I know about the case.

"But I will explain now why I'm taking you along, Kittow. Although local forces expect only one or two Yard people when they ask for our help, I have a feeling there will be a lot of people to see and a lot of paperwork. One never knows what officers the local force is able, or willing, to provide."

Kittow, who had no 'away case' experience, fervently hoped his inclusion in the investigation would be a positive one.

Bryce turned the Wolseley into Haig's street, and pulled up outside number 52 within a minute of the time he had mentioned the evening before. Climbing out of the car, he walked towards the house as the front door opened and a small girl came rushing towards him, throwing her arms around his legs. Grinning, he reached down and took one of the child's hands and walked her back up the path.

"'Morning, Fiona," Bryce greeted Rosie's mother at the door. "Sorry to drag Alex away from you both, again."

"Och, I understand, Mr Bryce, it's the job. Rosie has been waiting by the window since she got up this morning and we told her you were coming. She hasnae seen you very often, but you're definitely her favourite 'uncle'!"

Bryce wondered if he was perhaps popular because on previous occasions he had given the child some spending money. Being childless himself so far, and without any siblings to give him nieces and nephews, he rather liked to make an occasional fuss of someone else's offspring.

Fiona Haig caught sight of Kittow, now standing beside the car and stretching his legs and said in mild surprise "I see you have someone with you today."

Bryce called Kittow forward and introduced him. Kittow was astounded that the DCI knew and used his Christian name.

"Alex has mentioned you, Adam," said Fiona, "it's always nice to put a face to a name."

At this point Haig appeared at the door, carrying his bag. "'Morning guv; and 'morning to you too, Adam," he said. Noticing that his daughter was still clinging to his boss, he added "I hope you aren't going to spoil Rosie again today!"

Bryce looked down at the little girl and grinned again, "We must stick to precedent" he said, as he slid a half crown into a small palm and was rewarded with a shriek of pleasure.

Haig kissed his wife and daughter, and the three men went to the car.

On this journey, Kittow sat in the back, with the DCI again taking the wheel. For the first few miles Bryce was silent as he concentrated on driving. Haig half-turned towards Kittow and said:

"I wasnae expecting to see you today, Adam. What have you done to deserve this outing?"

"I dunno, Sarge," replied Kittow, "I was wondering myself. D'you reckon I've done something good or something bad?" he asked, beginning to doubt his earlier hope that he had been given an opportunity.

"Got to be something good, laddie, no question. Can't think the boss would introduce you to polite company in a mansion house if he wanted to punish you!"

Noticing the width of Bryce's smile at this remark, and the lines crinkling around his eye, Haig added "Of course, I have to hope the boss wouldnae trap me with you in a car and hotel for days on end to punish me, either!"

As their laughter subsided the Wolseley picked up speed along the A40, and Bryce was able to begin briefing his team.

"I've been given very little gen so far. When the Assistant Commissioner rang with the job, all I got was that there had been a poisoning during a wake, at what sounds like a stately home. The dead man is the priest, who had just conducted the funeral of the lady of the house.

"There were many, upwards of a hundred, guests present. Some were county notables; others were estate workers or local people. Unfortunately, when the man was taken ill the local doctor seems not to have recognised the symptoms of poison. It wasn't until the victim reached hospital that a more competent medic correctly diagnosed the problem. I've no idea what evidence will be left now."

Bryce continued with a criticism, "Communication has been poor. I expected further information at home last night, or to find a message had been telephoned through overnight to the Yard and left on my desk – but nothing. I don't even know the name of the victim. I have a book on country houses, and from that I learned that Mistram Manor belongs to a Colonel Hardwicke, but that's it. Anyway, we'll just have to see what we find."

"Should I get the road map out, and navigate, sir?" asked Haig.

"No need. I checked the route last night and it's very straightforward – far easier than that trip we made to Broughton in June."

"We'll have to play this by ear," said the DCI a few miles further on. "But the twin priorities are to see if any physical evidence remains of what the victim ate or drank; and to acquire a comprehensive list of those present yesterday.

"I'm assuming there will be someone from the local force available give us a bit of a briefing."

The three carried on a conversation about a recently concluded case for the next half hour, until Bryce turned off the main road. Following the sign-posted direction for Mistram, the car continued through a large village until wrought iron gates, with substantial lodges on either side, came into view.

"Unless there are two mansions in Mistram, I believe we've arrived, gentlemen," said Bryce as he stopped the car. "And judging by the quality of these lodges and gates, I think we can expect the house will also be rather exceptional."

The approach to the Mistram Manor estate was indeed impressive. Apart from their size, the lodges were beautifully designed mirror images, standing like magnificent bookends supporting the gates.

Surprisingly, there was no sign of life in either lodge. As the gates were standing open, the DCI put the car into gear again and started down the broad driveway. Mature poplars gave glimpses of lakes and rolling grounds, with extensive woodland beyond. After seven hundred yards or so they passed a church. A further two hundred yards and the drive opened out, the imposing front facade of the house now splendidly revealed.

"Aye, I'd say that's pretty grand," remarked Haig. He turned again to face Kittow, surprised that there had been no reaction from the back of the car. One look at the astonishment on the young detective's face explained his silence.

Bryce pulled the car up alongside an almost identical model. "Looks like there's a police presence here at the moment," he said. "Bring the murder bag from the boot, Kittow, and we'll go and introduce ourselves."

CHAPTER 5

Kittow re-joined his superiors as they approached the front door. The butler had posted a footman in the hall to watch for their arrival, and before the detectives had surmounted the final steps the footman had opened the front door, stepped outside, and quickly closed it again behind himself.

Sergeant Jarvis' entrance the previous day had more than discomfited Feeke. Whilst accepting that Jarvis had been absolutely correct in his approach, Feeke now considered that the formal notification of the murder had been given, and there was no need to admit any more policemen via the front door.

"Good morning, gentlemen," said the footman politely as the Yard men joined him on the broad threshold. "You'll be from Scotland Yard?" On receiving confirmation, he continued: "The Superintendent has just arrived, and is talking with Sergeant Jarvis and Mr Feeke in the servants' hall. If you would all follow me, please."

The three detectives trooped back down to the foot of the stone steps and found themselves led into a gap behind the steps themselves, and then through a cleverly concealed door. From here, they marched through a hallway and then into a large and very pleasant room, a spicey fragrance hanging in the air.

Seated at one end of an immense, scrubbed pine table, were a uniformed police superintendent, Sergeant Jarvis, and a man who, even without the statement of the footman, was clearly the butler.

The cook was standing by the range attending to a griddle filled with flat circles of spiced dough flecked with currants. A kitchen maid was laying plates, cups and saucers in front of each of the seated men, all of whom now rose to acknowledge the new arrivals.

Introductions performed, the visiting detectives were invited to take a seat at the table where the maid was already setting down the extra crockery.

"I shall inform Colonel Hardwicke that you are here," said Feeke standing up, "and that for the moment you are occupied discussing events with Superintendent Denton."

As the butler withdrew, the senior local officer made his intentions clear:

"I'll not stay long and get in your way, chief inspector. Sergeant Jarvis will give you such information as we have. I'm really here on behalf of the chief constable, to welcome you to the county, and to tell you that you can have whatever resources you may need. Beyond that, I can only wish you success with the investigation."

The superintendent lowered his head and blew gently on the tea which had just been put in front of him. By the uniform greyness of his full head of hair, and the liver spots which were forming on his hands, Bryce judged him to be in his mid-sixties. Denton continued:

"Although we've allocated Jarvis to assist you and your men, you should know he's been up all night. When he's briefed you perhaps you'll let him go home and get a bit of shuteye."

"Thank you, Superintendent." Turning to Jarvis Bryce said in a friendly tone:

"We certainly shan't detain you any longer than we need to, sergeant, so the sooner you tell us what you can, the sooner you can get to bed!"

The maid completed delivery of the remaining cups of tea, and then brought a fresh pot to the table so that second cups could be individually poured. Cook set down a platter of the warm, golden discs, together with a butter dish.

"There's nothing like fresh Welsh cakes and fresh butter," she said. "I only wish I could be a little more open-handed with the currants, but I know you'll all understand why not, and make allowances for me!"

Accepting simultaneous thanks from the

five men, both women smiled and left, closing the door quietly behind them.

Sergeant Jarvis wasn't the fastest thinker but, fortified by tea and Welsh cakes, he managed to present the limited information he possessed in a logical order. He started off in the approved manner by giving the victim's particulars, and the suggestion that strychnine was believed to be the lethal substance. He followed this with a fair outline of events as far as he knew them, explaining that he had been in the churchyard but hadn't gone on to the manor for the wake.

Jarvis also reported Colonel Hardwicke's suspicions and locking of the doors. Producing the keys as he spoke, he pushed them over the table to the DCI.

That the scene had been so quickly preserved was news to both Bryce and Denton. Bryce privately acknowledged the perspicacity of the host. The sergeant concluded with the colonel's promise to record the names of all those present yesterday, after which Jarvis ground to a halt.

Considering he had been on duty all night, Bryce thought he had put his report together quite well. The sergeant didn't say (and Bryce would never learn) that he had in fact managed almost five hours' sleep on the Chesterfield.

"Very good, thank you," said Bryce. "As Mr Denton has said, you go and get some rest now. I suggest you come back here at four, and we'll see what else you can do."

Jarvis left via the back door, and Denton stood up at the same time. "Just a couple of other things and I'll be off as well," he said. "The rector wasn't married, but his brother is coming from Oxford later this morning to identify the body, which is in the hospital mortuary – not sure if you'll want to see it yourself. The PM is fixed for two o'clock this afternoon, and naturally you can have someone there to observe if you wish." He passed a piece of paper to Bryce. "I've put the police station and my home telephone numbers down for you. You must call me if you need anything.

"Finally, you're billeted at the Dog and Partridge in the village. I only reserved two rooms, but I'll stop on my way back and arrange a third. I don't anticipate any problem."

"Thank you for all that, sir," said Bryce. "I'll keep you informed, of course."

With the Superintendent gone, the three detectives turned their attention back to the table. An interrogative glance at his colleagues while lifting the teapot produced enthusiastic nods for seconds from both his subordinates. With their cups refilled, Haig passed around the plate of still warm and delicious Welsh cakes again.

Feeke, meanwhile, was searching for his master. He had last seen the colonel leaving the dining room an hour earlier, as breakfast obviously couldn't be served in the usual room. He couldn't be in the locked parlour, where he was usually to be found reading the paper after breakfast. He wasn't to be found in the drawing room, library, or the study either. Feeke finally tracked him down in the gun room, where he was cleaning a shotgun, watched by his daughter and daughter-in-law.

"Sorry to disturb you sir, but three detectives have arrived from Scotland Yard. Cook is rustling up tea and something tasty for them."

Feeke, now found himself feeling even more discomfited than he had been the previous day when Sergeant Jarvis arrived. Without divulging his earlier front door-defending action to his master, he gave the colonel some necessary facts:

"I should say, sir, that the senior man, Chief Inspector Bryce, is in fact a rather distinguished gentleman. I've read something of his background in the papers. He was on the front pages again more recently in connection with the Marylebone Public Baths case."

"By Jove, yes, Feeke. I recall that too. He's a lawyer as well as a policeman, and a decorated soldier too – got a Military Cross. Sounds as though the Met has sent us their top man!

"You can say that again, Albert!" interjected Angela, looking highly delighted at Feeke's news. "Miles and I know him well – we were at his wedding in August! All three of us are members of the same Inn, although our training didn't overlap. I've also been involved in prosecuting a couple of his cases. The Bar's loss is undoubtedly Scotland

Yard's gain.

"Why don't I go along and see him first?" she suggested. "I saw a bit of what was happening in the parlour, so I can take him there and tell him who was standing where, and so on."

"Good idea," agreed Hardwicke, "When he's sized things up, presumably his men can carry on in there without him. If he has a few minutes, bring him along to the drawing room. He can pick my brains there, such as they are – and meet the rest of the family at the same time. Oh, and do tell him he can use the breakfast room or parlour as his base for the duration."

Turning back to the butler, Hardwicke said, "Feeke, my list of guests is on my desk in the study – please collect it and take it to Mr Bryce. Actually, I've been remiss – I meant to ask you and the staff to draw up a list yourselves, as it's quite possible my family and I have forgotten someone."

"I anticipated it might be helpful for the staff to make a list, sir, and we have already done so. I shall give ours to the Chief Inspector with yours, sir. However, I will admit we weren't quite sure of the names of all your friends, nor of some of the more distant relations, so the staff list is not likely to be as complete as yours."

Feeke left to carry out his master's request, but before Angela could follow him, Hardwicke raised a hand and stopped her. When the butler had shut the door he said:

"I realise that you and Esther both saw me

coming in here earlier, and either independently or jointly feared that I might be contemplating blowing my brains out. You should both know me better than that. Yes, I feel utterly drained, and my spirits are very low indeed at the moment; but please be reassured that I have not the remotest inclination to do away with myself!"

Esther gave her father a hug. She was a good-looking woman with the same lean and rangy build as her brother; but where Miles favoured his father's square jaw and Roman nose, Esther had inherited her mother's heart-shaped face and full lips.

"Sorry, father," she said. "You're right, of course. We saw you unlock the gun room door, and I suppose we both had the same horrid thought. So we felt we needed to check on you." Angela nodded her confirmation.

"Well, you must both put any such grimness out of your minds," Hardwicke reassured them. "It's not going to happen – ever. I used this gun earlier on the day your mother died, and things being what they were, I locked it away without cleaning it. Today, I remembered, and thought I should make an effort to pick up the rest of my life where I left off."

He returned the 12-bore to its cabinet and all three left the gun room, Hardwicke locking the door behind them.

Esther and her father turned towards the drawing room, and Angela walked along the corridor in the opposite direction through the green baize door into the kitchen and servants' hall. On entering, the three detectives politely rose.

"Good heavens!" said Bryce, the sudden and unexpected appearance of his friend taking him completely by surprise. Angela moved quickly round the table, swung her plump arms around him and planted a most affectionate kiss on his cheek.

Realising that this display needed explaining to his subordinates, Bryce recovered rapidly and introduced Angela to an equally surprised Haig and Kittow:

"This is Miss Lacon, who sometimes prosecutes at the Old Bailey and elsewhere."

To Angela he said "I knew your married name was Hardwicke, of course, but it's not an uncommon name and it never crossed my mind that you and Miles might be connected to this house!"

"Well, as you've now worked out, the connection is that Miles is Colonel Hardwicke's son. Do sit down and finish your tea as we chat, gentlemen."

Angela settled herself in a chair beside the DCI. "Of course, Miles and I weren't married at Mistram – we were married from my parents' place in Devon. So you wouldn't even have seen this address on your invitation. But if you'd been able to come to our wedding in 1938 you would have met Albert and Beth, naturally."

"Yes, I was disappointed to miss your nuptials. I remember I was away on my annual two-week territorial service, and I'd been sent to Hong Kong on an army exercise. And of course the war was in full swing for Isla and Ben's christenings too, so another missed opportunity to meet your wider family."

Haig and Kittow both listened with interest to these snippets of their chief's former life. Independently, each man formed a favourable impression of Miss Lacon, Kittow being particularly drawn to her unaffected manner and ready smile.

"Philip, my father-in-law has asked that you come along and speak to him – and other members of the family – after you've got started in the parlour, that is," said Angela. "But I've come first to try and help. I was acting as hostess in the breakfast room and parlour, where the rector was taken ill, so I'm probably better placed to describe who was present than anyone else in the house. I assume Jarvis has given you the keys?"

"Yes, he has." However, the unexpected pleasure of meeting his old friend was ebbing very quickly for Bryce, and he shared his concerns:

"Delighted as I am to see you, the fact that you and Miles are here is obviously problematic for me. I'll have to consult with the Chief Constable and my Assistant Commissioner. It will be for them to say whether they think my position remains tenable, or if they believe I'm irrevocably compromised because of our friendship."

Sergeant Haig looked most put out to hear this possibility. He enjoyed working with Bryce as much as he enjoyed the fact that their partnership was increasingly recognised as a successful one. The idea of the DCI leaving – whilst he and Kittow stayed on to work with a replacement, did not find favour with him; not least because there was more than one detective inspector at the Yard that he wouldn't want to ever work with again. He hoped the top brass would rule that his boss could continue.

"However," Bryce continued, "I can see no reason why I shouldn't at least inspect the principal rooms involved and get the investigation started, pending a decision from on high. So lead on please, Angie, and show us the sights."

As they got up from the table the butler came back bearing some sheets of paper, which he handed to the DCI.

"The colonel asked me to give you his list of guests from yesterday, sir. I also took the liberty of preparing a list with all the staff, but as I explained to the colonel, we didn't know the names of all the visitors."

"Thank you, Feeke," replied Bryce.

"I can tell you now, Philip," said Angela, as her friend folded the papers and slipped them into the inside pocket of his jacket, "that all the immediate family – including the four grandchildren – joined in with the production of

Albert's list. Still no guarantee it's complete, of course."

She led the three policemen out of the servants' quarters and into the main house corridor. Crossing the hall at a brisk pace she paused when she reached the breakfast room door, realising that instead of footsteps following behind her, there was now silence. Turning back, she found that all three detectives had stopped to take in the detail of the manor's spectacular entrance.

There was a great deal of detail to see. Eight, huge columns – cleverly painted to match the marble floor and staircase – were arranged to form an octagon around the room, all supporting an ornate ceiling high above.

In between six of the spaces created by the columns stood six, oval, gilt tables. Each of these supported either a large bust of an earlier Hardwicke, or a beautiful bronze of horses in various poses.

The walls behind the tables were painted in a pale moss green (the perfect foil for the white and pink-veined marble) and hung with enormous gilt-framed oil paintings depicting scenes of the estate – St Anselm's immediately recognisable in one.

The seventh side of the octagon was filled by the front door, the tracery of its beautiful fanlight repeated in the soaring, full-height windows on either side. Immediately opposite the door was the central table, beside which the colonel had stood the day before, and beyond that a magnificent marble staircase completed the octagon. Sweeping upwards before splitting into galleried landings, its moss green carpet held back with gleaming brass rods, the staircase was the final breathtaking aspect of the hall.

Haig, noticing Kittow in open-mouthed amazement beside him, whispered "Are you catching flies there, laddie?"

Kittow, whose parents and younger siblings had been bombed out of their humble two up/two down, now lived in a prefabricated bungalow on the Excalibur estate in Catford. With the acute shortage of housing after the war they were all very glad to have been allocated a prefab home. But he couldn't help wondering how many similar prefabs could be stacked up in the reception hall alone. He dearly wished his mother could see all that he was experiencing at Mistram Manor. He snapped his jaws together again just as Angela returned.

"All rather astonishing, isn't it?" she said with a smile for the young detective constable. "Although I have to confess, as much as I love it here, I'm always pleased to go back to the house in Holland Park – so much more manageable as a family home!"

Kittow shyly returned her smile. He had no doubt what she said was true. But, having walked a beat in Holland Park earlier in his career, he suspected that Miss Lacon's home would still be large and magnificent.

They all moved on again, Angela indicating a door a little way ahead:

"The parlour is that room further along – you have the key to that as well, Philip, although it's temporarily blocked on the other side. I'll take you to it through the breakfast room, here. The dining room, like the hall, has been cleared. As far as anyone knows, the rector never went into the dining room, and he only spent moments in the hall when he first arrived."

Bryce drew from his pocket the keys which Jarvis had given him. In accordance with a well-known 'law', the first key didn't fit. Trying the second, he unlocked and opened the door. Then, standing in the wide doorway, he spent a full minute taking in the scene.

The room was not quite square, measuring perhaps thirty feet by twenty-seven feet. The large, centrally positioned table, held dirty plates and glasses, as well as crumpled up napkins and empty bottles. Dining chairs had been pulled out from under the table and positioned in groups around the room, many to take advantage of the view of the gardens. Against the wall on either side of the door were two huge mahogany buffets. Serving plates, still with various food items, were spread out on these. At both ends of the room were smaller tables, each with supplies of different drinks.

One wall was dominated by the interconnecting doors, still closed as the colonel had left them. Bryce guessed they would provide an opening of about fifteen feet into the parlour. The DCI stepped towards these doors, calling over his shoulder as he went that Haig should start taking photographs of the breakfast room, with Kittow observing and learning the skill.

Bryce found the parlour was a room of the same width as the breakfast room, but perhaps a few feet longer. Like the breakfast room, the windows provided views of the gardens.

The parlour was nevertheless a surprise. The rest of the house so far was quintessentially 'old England'. The parlour, however, was entirely furnished and decorated in a very different style. Exquisitely embellished red and black lacquered furniture filled the room, interspersed with beautiful oriental rugs. An extraordinary collection of *famille rose* oriental ceramics was displayed – rather over-crowdedly – on top of four large cabinets in the room. Bryce, admiring a pair of moon flasks, correctly assumed that a number of the beautiful pieces had been temporarily repositioned from occasional tables in the room. Instead of the portraits and landscapes hanging elsewhere in the house, the walls of the parlour held framed silk embroideries and fans; each example clearly selected to complement the china and rugs.

There were no serving plates in here. The

half dozen or so small, lacquered tables, and a larger table pushed against the wall in front of the door to the corridor, were all well-covered with protective cloths, and still held a few empty plates and glasses. Although now in a disarranged and oddly reconfigured state, Bryce could see that the parlour was a delightful room, normally providing comfort and peace for its occupants.

Behind him, Angela said "Albert and Beth loved this room – I believe they used it after breakfast almost every day when there were no guests."

"It's certainly a fine room," said Bryce. "Anyway, back to business I'm afraid, Angie. Show me where you were standing, please; where the rector was, and as far as you can remember who else was in here and where they were standing. I need to know from the time you first saw the rector come in, to the time he collapsed. I appreciate that you couldn't be watching him and his group all the time, of course, but an outline will help no end."

"I think the best thing will be if I draw a plan later, marking each person as best I can, but in the meantime I'll tell you all I can remember."

"Just the job," replied the DCI.

"Well, I stood about a yard away from the doors, just inside the breakfast room." Angela moved back to show the position. "I could see most of the parlour – I couldn't see part of the cabinet to the left, nor a bit of the room to the right. But I could clearly see the main table by the parlour door where Simeon was standing, and all of the chairs.

"Simeon stood within reach of the table, facing me. By 'within reach' I mean that he wasn't actually touching the table – anyone could have passed between him and it, and I'm certain people did. But he could have set his plate or glass down on the table without really having to move. Being tall, he had a long reach.

"I can tell you for certain, Philip, that he took up that position from the moment he came through from the breakfast room with his plate. Actually, he was almost the last person to go through to the parlour – I think only the other cleric came into the room after him. Most of the earliest arrivals in the breakfast room took their food out to eat in the hall. At least four people went to sit in the easy chairs, and they were followed by others. That left perhaps eight or nine people around that far side and corner of the table who, like me, chose to stand throughout the wake. They were already formed into a sort of group, which Simeon joined."

Angela paused to reflect, then continued, "Once Simeon arrived, as far as I saw he stayed put. I suppose it was the best part of forty minutes from the time he came in, to the time he collapsed."

Bryce nodded, a picture was forming very clearly in his mind, and he thanked Angela for her help.

"If you would make your plan, naming the eight or nine people you mentioned who were standing by the rector, that would be most helpful. I'll come along to the drawing room in a little while. I take it there's no objection to my using the telephone?"

"Of course not. You'll find one in the hall, and Albert has said that you can base yourself in the parlour or breakfast room," replied Angela, and with another smile for the DCI she went off to look for paper and a pencil.

CHAPTER 6

His friend gone, Bryce spent a few more minutes reviewing what he had been told and then returned to his subordinates.

"Haig, when you're done in here, detailed photographs of the parlour, please. Make sure your pictures show the position of every single item of crockery and glassware. Then show Kittow how to bag up and label the bits and pieces. Concentrate entirely on what is left on the largest table where the rector was standing first – not forgetting that glass on the floor underneath.

"We have to wait for cause of death to be confirmed formally, of course, but as Jarvis told us this morning, strychnine has been mentioned. From the symptoms described, it sounds like an acute attack, not a case of small doses. If that's right, it seems almost certain that the rector swallowed it at the table in the parlour.

"Kittow, if in doubt about something, ask Sergeant Haig. I'm going to take soundings now as to whether I can continue here."

Bryce went back through the corridor to the hall to use the telephone. The instrument was on a small table, a chair placed conveniently alongside. With a clear view of both corridors, he would easily spot anyone approaching who might overhear him – not that there was anything particularly confidential about this call.

Picking up the instrument, he gave the operator the private number for Scotland Yard. Once connected, he identified himself, and asked to be put through to the Assistant Commissioner (Crime). After getting past the AC's secretary/gatekeeper, he was eventually able to speak to the man himself. In a few brief sentences, he outlined the dilemma.

"Unusual situation, certainly," remarked his superior. "I know Angela Lacon, of course – Miles Hardwicke too, slightly. When Oxford rang asking for help, the Hardwicke name wasn't mentioned, but although I knew Miles comes from a landed family, even if the name had been given I probably still wouldn't have made the connection. It's not an unusual name, after all.

"Anyway, I assume you have numerous suspects. Is there any reason to think that any of the immediate family is involved?"

"None at all, so far, sir," replied Bryce. "But my investigation has barely started, and if that should change at any point as matters progress, I should immediately withdraw from the case."

To which he added with deep feeling, "Frankly, I shouldn't want to be involved in pursuing a friend, or a member of their family, on a capital charge!"

"Is it likely that you could come under undue pressure to take the investigation in a particular direction, or avoid asking pertinent questions?"

"Absolutely not, sir," replied the DCI firmly.

"I see. Very well, then. I'll talk to the Oxfordshire Chief Constable, with my recommendation that you carry on. Unless he demurs, in which case I'll get a message to you pronto, you should assume that you remain in charge, Bryce. Just let me have your number there."

Happier, but still wishing this complication hadn't arisen, the DCI returned to the breakfast room. He reported on the conversation, and was heartened to see both Haig and Kittow were visibly pleased that the AC had not removed him. While the officers were having a brief discussion about how best to transport the evidence, they heard the telephone ring. Shortly after, the butler arrived:

"A telephone call for you, chief inspector," he reported.

"Thank you Feeke," said Bryce. Returning to the hall to as before, he took up the instrument and the butler discreetly disappeared.

"Bryce here... Oh, yes, sir...Well, I appreciate that...Thank you very much...Yes, I'll certainly do that...Goodbye."

He hung the earpiece back on its stand.

Returning to the parlour he told his colleagues: "It's confirmed – I'm staying,"

A spontaneous 'hurrah' came from both men, which made him smile.

"Right, carry on here while I talk to the family. If you both leave for any reason, lock the breakfast room door behind you." Bryce gave Haig the key and went off again, this time to find the drawing room.

As directed, he passed the parlour door, then the study door. A further forty feet or so of blank wall followed before he arrived at a door straight ahead of him at the end of the corridor. He tapped firmly on this, and opened it.

The adults of the family sat on sofas grouped around a low table. Bryce immediately recognised his friend Miles sitting beside his wife. A spruce elderly man, dressed exactly in the manner of a country squire albeit with a black armband, stood up and extended his hand:

"Albert Hardwicke. Delighted to meet you, chief inspector, although naturally, I should have preferred your first visit to be under very different circumstances.

"I understand you know Miles and Angela, so let me introduce my son-in-law Henry Ainscough, and my daughter Esther."

Bryce shook the hand extended by Lord Ainscough and saw an agreeable-looking man in his late thirties. He was struck by how similar Henry was in appearance to Angela. It seemed that

Miles and Esther had both chosen spouses who were their physical opposites – Henry and Angela sharing shorter, plumper frames, and both with dark wavy hair.

The courtesies completed, Hardwicke addressed his son-in-law: "Henry, you're nearest the bell; will you ring, please, and we'll have some coffee.

"It's one of my disappointments in life that since they've grown up neither my son nor my daughter ever brings their friends to Mistram. We've never actually discussed this topic, although I've told them often enough that we have plenty of space. I hope it isn't that my children think that their mother and I were inhospitable."

Esther laughed. "Not at all, father. I probably speak for Miles as well if I say that the main reason we have been wary ever since leaving school and going out into the world, is that the way of life here might be difficult for our friends to assimilate. True, I'm married to a very affluent peer of the realm, but even now most of our circle are upper-middle class, don't dress for dinner, and have comparatively little money."

"Fair enough," he said, "it's true that your mother and I were sticklers for the old conventions when it came to entertaining. I can understand why you youngsters would prefer to relax things a little.

"Anyway, chief inspector, perhaps after breaking the ice this visit you might agree to return at a later date as my guest."

Before Bryce could make any reply, Feeke appeared in the room, and Hardwicke issued instructions to bring plenty of coffee, and "something to go with it."

After the butler left, Hardwicke said:

"With my wife gone, those in this room now, plus my grandchildren, are my immediate family. I have no other direct relations except a handful of cousins of one degree or another. They – and Beth's own sister and her husband – were here yesterday, of course."

"Our two children, and Miles' two, are playing upstairs," explained Henry. "They've all been allowed the rest of the week off before they return to school."

"Yes," said the colonel. "I imagine you'll want to talk to everyone who might have seen anything significant, Bryce, and my grandchildren were certainly roving about between the rooms yesterday. So perhaps you should talk to them this afternoon before they have a chance to forget something which might not be important to them?"

"I expect you're intending to order us all to stay in the house," laughed Angela.

"A bit late for that," smiled Bryce. I gather yesterday's guests are already spread out around the country. And I agree, Colonel; in my experience kids sometimes notice things that an adult might not – and their memories tend to be pretty good, too. So yes, I'd like to talk to the children.

"I do need to speak to each of you as well, of course. Now this is a delicate matter, but I'll be very blunt. Everyone who was in the house yesterday, including all of you, must be considered in the list of possible suspects. That being so, I know you'll appreciate that I need to talk to each of you individually. Miles and Angie will know the risks involved in allowing one suspect to hear the story being told by another!"

Everyone laughed, although all fully understood the serious point the DCI was making.

"I haven't yet had a chance to look at the two guest lists that have been produced. For the moment, I'm going to concentrate on those whom we know were around Mr Watson after he arrived in the parlour.

"By the way, I don't know if Angie has told you, but I had no inkling that she and Miles were connected with this house until I arrived here and saw her. As soon as I realised that she and Miles were 'on the list', my first thought was that I should withdraw – recuse myself, as our American friends would say – and suggest that a more independent officer should take charge. However, I've spoken to the Assistant Commissioner in London, and to the Chief Constable here. Both have expressed their belief that I will be able to investigate 'without fear or favour, affection or ill-will,' exactly as my oath requires."

A maid, escorted by the butler, arrived

with the coffee. When this had been poured and distributed, Bryce continued.

"Anyway, colonel, my condolences on the loss of your wife. And also of a man whom I imagine was a friend as well as priest."

Hardwicke shook his head, apparently reluctant to accept the DCI's last comment without some qualification. "As a parish priest I'd say he was first-class. Took services even when he was ill and should have been in bed; visited the sick; sorted the choir; the organists; and the roster for flower arranging; organised fetes; and quite a bit more besides."

Hardwicke gulped down some coffee and continued:

"And yes, Watson was a regular guest here, and dined with Beth and me perhaps once a month. But I shouldn't exactly describe him as a friend. The dinner invitations were really to the holder of his office, rather than to him as a friend or relation. I'll be the first to admit that he and I didn't always see eye-to-eye about ritual, or liturgical or canonical matters, or whatever the technical term is, but we can talk about that when we have our *tete-a-tete* later."

"Yes indeed," said Bryce. "However, there is one thing I'd like cleared up at this stage. I understand that after the rector was taken away in the ambulance, you expressed doubt about the doctor's provisional diagnosis – to the extent that you ordered the breakfast room and the parlour to be sealed, effectively. I'm immensely grateful to you for that quick action, of course, but I'd just like to hear why you thought to do it."

"Instinct, I suppose. I was in the hall when Doreen cried out, although I didn't know who it was at the time. I sent Feeke to investigate. He returned and reported that Watson had collapsed, and described the symptoms – as they had been told to him. Hearsay, in other words.

"So I went to see for myself. On the way in, I spoke to two old friends, both experienced soldiers. They pointedly queried Dr Ford's competence. By the time I saw Watson he was mercifully unconscious – Ford said he'd administered a strong sedative. I could only look at Watson's face."

The colonel swallowed several more gulps of coffee. "I lay no claim to having any medical training," he said as he replaced his cup in its saucer. "But in the last fifty or so years I have seen cases involving all four of the alternative diagnoses that Ford suggested. None of his options completely matched the reported facts, in my opinion. That was the point at which I thought it was some form of poisoning, and perhaps deliberate.

"Angie was with me, so she will give you her recollections. But to my mind, even if it was nothing worse than food poisoning, it seemed sensible to lock the rooms and to keep everyone out. At that stage I still hoped, of course, that

Watson would recover, and that there was some simple explanation."

"Yes, that's quite correct, Philip," said Angela. "Incidentally, I concur completely with Albert's reasoning. I didn't know it would turn out to be deliberate, but I certainly thought some form of poisoning was infinitely more likely than any of Brian Ford's options."

"Thank you," replied Bryce, thinking carefully. "Now, how far have you got with your plan of the parlour, Angie?"

"I've done a first draft for you – it's on that table," she pointed to a console by the door. "I'm ready to talk you through it."

"Good – let's go and discuss it now, if you'll excuse us, colonel."

"Of course, my dear chap, you must come and go as you wish. I hope Angie told you that you can use the breakfast room or the parlour as your base. On reflection, however, neither is particularly convenient – still evidence in there and the breakfast room, I suppose, and also there is no telephone. I suggest you take over my study instead, and you can lock the door. It won't inconvenience me. But, when you've finished with the other rooms, perhaps you'll let me know – I like to use the parlour.

"Oh, and another thing. I imagine you won't agree to have lunch or dinner with us, but I'll arrange with Feeke and Cook that you and your men only have to ring for whatever food or drink you fancy, and it'll be brought to you. No strychnine included," he ended rather lamely.

"Much appreciated, colonel," replied Bryce, "and one final point. When I've extracted all of Angie's information from her, I'd like to talk to you next. Then a brief chat with the children – possibly, and, contrary to what I said before about separate interviews, that might be best done in a group. A parent can obviously be present, of course.

"After that, I'll have to play it by ear, but from what I've learned so far, you Miles, and your sister and brother-in-law, weren't around the rector at any time. Obviously, you won't be in the priority list of interviewees – not sure if that'll be a relief or a disappointment for you!"

Bryce and Angela left the room, collecting her sketch plan on the way.

"If you would go ahead to the study, Angie, I'll join you there after I see how my men are doing."

CHAPTER 7

Bryce continued through the hall, and then into the parlour via the breakfast room. Haig and Kittow were busy sorting out various piles of potential evidence, of which there was a substantial quantity.

"I got the butler to find us some boxes and bags, sir," reported Haig. "It's going to be quite a job to get all this stuff back to Hendon."

"Good thinking," replied Bryce, eyeing the amount which had been accumulated so far. "Keep going, and then we'll see if we maybe need to hire a van of some sort to take this lot back to London. I'm just going to talk to Miss Lacon, who has drawn up a plan identifying, I hope, who was around the victim. It may be that we can thin out some of this material, so that less needs to be sent to the lab.

"Incidentally, regarding my friendship with two of the family here, which is a longstanding one as you must have realised, it obviously isn't an ideal situation. So, I want to make something very clear to you both." The serious tone of the DCI's voice wasn't lost on his subordinates, both of whom were now looking more intently at him. "If either of you has even the slightest suspicion about anyone in this household – from the colonel down – you voice it immediately. Is that clear?"

Instant acknowledgement from both men satisfied Bryce that his point had been well understood and, if need arose, would be acted upon. In a lighter tone he asked Haig:

"Now, can Kittow be trusted to carry on here, while you and I hear what Miss Lacon has to tell us?"

"Oh aye, sir – he actually shows promise," replied Haig, to Kittow's relief.

The two officers joined Angela in the study. This was a man's room, without a doubt. A large desk with tooled, burgundy leather inlay, was the principal piece of furniture, with a comfortable swivel chair for the colonel. Two upright chairs in the same burgundy leather faced the desk. A few filing cabinets, and bookcases mostly bearing reference works, stood against the walls, with photographs of various dogs and some sporting prints hanging above and beside them. The herringbone wood floor had no rugs, and the plain, dark blue velvet curtains at the windows fell straight to the floor without the tiebacks and pelmet treatments in other rooms.

Moving around to join Angela behind the desk, where she had spread out her diagram, Bryce saw a single framed photograph stood on the green leather. A semi-formal shot of the colonel and his late wife, together with his children and grandchildren.

The three sat down around the desk, Angela taking the colonel's chair. Using a pencil as a pointer, she started to describe the scene to the two men.

"As I said earlier, Philip, there was already a little group at the far end of the parlour before Simeon arrived. He stood, with his plate and glass either in his hand or on the table – always within reach. Once there, I don't recall any of them came back to the breakfast room to replenish glasses or plates – presumably they all took a large enough first helping. A few minutes after Simeon arrived, another clergyman went in. But after him, over the thirty or forty minutes that I was there I don't remember anyone else joining the group.

"There were three incidents which may be significant, but let me just detail the individuals, and I'll come back to those in a minute.

"These were the people in the group, to the best of my recollection." She pointed to her diagram, which showed the position of table and chairs, with numbered dots representing people. At the bottom of the plan was a key, allocating a name to each number.

"Number One is Simeon, of course. He was facing in my direction practically every time I looked; numbers two, three, and four were really behind him.

"Although yesterday I got the impression that there was a single conversation centred on Simeon, when I came to sketch the plan I realised that it's quite possible that what seemed to be a single large group might well have had two or more conversations going at the same time. Probably did, in fact, given the numbers congregating there. Because Simeon was so tall, he seemed to be the focal point, but that might have been an illusion."

"I see that," said Bryce, "we'll just take it that the people you mention were in that vicinity, not necessarily directly involved with the rector."

"Anyway, there were two people around Simeon that I didn't know. One was a man I assumed to be a farmer; the other was the young man in a clerical collar. Last night when the family was drawing up the list of attendees, I described them and Albert immediately said the first one was Silas Anderson from New Farm, one of his tenant farmers. Albert described him as an 'excellent fellow'.

"The other was John Edwards, one of Beth's obscure relations – third cousin once removed, or something. He's a curate in London somewhere. Albert said he'd only been to Mistram a few times, for lunch – I gather he'd never stayed in the house. Albert gave him a much less glowing appraisal – 'ingratiating, grovelling little man'. He said that now Beth's gone he won't be invited again."

She paused for a moment, staring at her plan, and mentally transporting herself back to the previous day.

"Anyway, the rest of the group around the rector were all people that I know, at least slightly. There was Bixby, a gardener; Travis McKay, Albert's solicitor; James Dauntsey, the land agent; Major Hicks, one of Albert's very oldest friends; Marcus Eccles, the landlord of the Dog and Partridge; and Doreen, a housemaid."

Bryce looked up from the plan. "We'll be staying with Mr Eccles tonight," he said. "What are he and his hostelry like?"

"It's a nice enough place, well-run – at least in the saloon bar. He's one of Albert's tenants, of course, like most of the villagers. I'm not a beer drinker, but Miles and Henry say that Eccles knows how to keep his ale. I've never stayed overnight, so I can't answer for the rooms. His wife was also in the parlour, but she was sitting by the window, talking to Mrs Wilkin, the postmistress."

Angela stopped, and looked at the two men. Neither spoke, both still staring down at the plan.

"Our initial problem, Angie, is that as yet we haven't officially been told what killed the rector. But if we work on the assumption that the hospital's belief that it was strychnine is correct, then that immediately throws up another question – how was it ingested?"

"Yes, I'm sufficiently familiar with poisons to know that strychnine is so horrible-tasting that it would need to be disguised, unlike say arsenic which might have been added to anything."

"You said you had three incidents to tell us about, ma'am," prompted Haig.

"Oh, yes, sergeant; sorry. At one point quite early on there must have been a lull in the conversation in both rooms, because I actually heard Simeon say to Doreen – using what I can only describe as his pulpit voice – 'I know you are off duty, Doreen, but go through and fetch me a glass of red wine'. She came past me to fetch it for him."

"So, Angie, we can put you near the top of the list of 'those with opportunity'," said Bryce.

"Yes indeed, Philip. But you'll find it pretty hard to ascribe a motive – and although someone presumably managed to find the means, I can honestly say that I wouldn't know where to start!

"The second incident involves my daughter, Isla. She and Ben were in the breakfast room, sometimes sitting at the table, sometimes moving around. You know them well, Philip, and you know they aren't shy. They knew several of the guests anyway. At one point I saw Isla take a glass of wine out towards the hall. I didn't say anything, as I know she detests wine, so I knew she wasn't slipping out to have a drink herself! I assumed she was taking it to someone by request. That was correct – last night Albert told me that she brought it out for him. When I asked Isla about it this morning, she said that one of the 'old men' by the door suggested it to her – that would have been one of the two generals standing close to the drinks table.

"But I'm digressing. The key point is this: later, as Isla was moving around, Simeon probably saw she wasn't carrying a plate or glass herself, and called out in a voice again loud enough for me to hear: 'Isla, be a good girl and fetch me a cup of black coffee'.

"Now, I have to confess that I was distracted for a minute, and I didn't see whether Isla actually poured the coffee herself, or if someone nearby did the pouring. I imagine the latter. That's something you'll have to ask her yourself. But I certainly saw her take the coffee back to Simeon.

"The third thing is that Albert himself came in for a few minutes, and chatted to the group. That was after Doreen fetched the wine, but he'd gone again before Isla brought the coffee."

There was a silence for a minute, as all three considered the implications. Eventually the DCI spoke.

"As the sergeant here knows, in all cases I treat everyone involved as a suspect, until someone else has been charged and convicted.

"Even I, however, am happy to eliminate Isla from the list of suspects. Provisionally, you too, Angie, as your point about motive does seem compelling," he added with a smile. "And although I'll reserve judgement until I've seen the maid, she doesn't seem a very likely suspect either.

"Given that red wine – or even better, coffee

– would serve towards disguising the bitterness of strychnine, there must be a possibility that the poison was somehow added to one or the other. If it's the coffee, then your father-in-law is eliminated too. And, of course, it goes in his favour that he made the decision to preserve the scene – which he didn't have to do."

He thought again for a moment. "Too many people," he muttered, almost to himself. "Not just the people standing around the victim – but an unknown number of others between him and the drinks tables.

"One last question. The obvious one. Do you know of anyone who might have any reason to kill the rector?"

"To kill him, no, absolutely not. We discussed this briefly, just before you came through to the drawing room earlier. You'll have to talk to Albert, and to Miles and Esther, as they have more direct knowledge, but I understand Simeon hasn't always gone out of his way to court popularity. He's had what might be called 'spats' with several of the locals – and with Albert, as you heard a few minutes ago. Actually, I believe it's been suggested that he may have had two different personalities. But from what I've heard, there's nothing remotely sufficient to be a motive for murder. Assuming the poison was intended to kill, of course."

"Right," said Bryce; "I need to change the witness order I'd provisionally decided. But excuse

DEATH AT MISTRAM MANOR

me a second while I make a call."

Picking up the telephone on the desk, he gave the number which Denton had given him earlier. Eventually getting through, Bryce asked where the autopsy was to be held. Receiving the answer, he asked the superintendent to inform the police surgeon that a Yard officer would attend the PM to observe, and ended the call with his thanks.

"First, though, I think we'd better take up your father-in-law's kind offer of food." He pressed the bell push which was conveniently near the desk.

Within a minute, Feeke appeared. "You rang, sir?"

"Yes; two things, Feeke. Roughly how long would it take to drive to Lambert Street? And is it easy to find?"

"From here, sir, about twenty minutes, but best to allow a bit of time for parking. Say half an hour. It's very easy to find, sir. The main road into town becomes High Street, and Lambert Street is the third turning off on the left. If it's the mortuary you are after, it's about a hundred yards along on the right."

"Excellent, thank you. Now, Colonel Hardwicke very kindly offered Mrs Jeff's services, to provide my men and me with some food. Would you please ask if she could find something very simple for three, as soon as possible?"

"Certainly, sir. I believe Cook has already begun to sort something out in anticipation of your request. Lady Ainscough spoke to her about it earlier. Will you be joining the officers yourself, madam?

"No, I think not, Feeke – they will no doubt want to 'talk shop' without a suspect present," replied Angela.

"Thank you, Feeke: and we'll eat in here I think, to avoid mixing today's lunch with yesterday's leftovers."

"Sergeant, fetch Kittow in here, would you. Make sure you lock the breakfast room door behind you.

"Now, Angie, when we've had a bite to eat, I'd like to talk to Isla and Doreen. Was Ben with Isla during the coffee incident?"

"Well, partly. At that time, he was with Jeremy Waites at the end of the breakfast room furthest from the parlour, which is where the coffee pots were standing. Waites is the head gamekeeper, and he has a remarkable range of grotesque facial expressions – gurning, really – which I've seen him demonstrate before. Ideal entertainment for a seven-year-old boy!"

"Okay; I'll probably see him later, but it doesn't seem likely he can add anything to Isla's report.

"So, would you bring Isla here at about two o'clock – assuming the family has finished lunch by then? You'll stay with her, of course, and Miles can be present too, if you wish."

"Don't be ridiculous, Philip. She's known you

all her life, albeit you were away for a lot of her first five years, and she's very fond of you. You're an honorary uncle, in fact. If Miles and I aren't there she'll be far more natural, not worrying she might be going to annoy us by saying the wrong thing. No doubt you'll have more questions for me later, but I'll go now, and bring Isla along at two."

"Fair enough, Angie, thanks. I'll hear Isla first, and then see Doreen afterwards. Would you mind giving your father-in-law my apologies, and say that I've pushed him down the batting order a bit?"

CHAPTER 8

Haig and Kittow arrived as Angela left the room.

"Sit down, both of you," instructed Bryce.

Kittow, finding the only remaining chair was the colonel's, sat down in it somewhat self-consciously.

"First, we're about to be brought something to eat. After that, Kittow, I want you to take the car and observe the *post mortem*, to be held in the Lambert Street mortuary at two o'clock. You'll need to leave here by one thirty at the latest – best make it one fifteen" Bryce relayed Feeke's directions. "Have you seen a PM before?"

"No sir. But I saw a lot of dead and blown-up bodies after I was called up in the last year of the war. Can't think a PM will be a worse experience."

"Fair enough. Be sure to take the bag with you, and get Watson's prints before the autopsy starts – we may need them to identify a cup or something.

"Now, it seems that the victim was brought a

glass of red wine by a housemaid who was present, and a cup of black coffee by Miss Lacon's nine-year-old daughter. Either medium seems more suitable for hiding the flavour of strychnine than any of the food. So, as soon as you return, go back into the parlour. Concentrate on preserving glasses on the parlour table which contain or might have contained red wine, and cups which might have contained black coffee.

"While you're at the morgue, we'll try to find out from Isla and Doreen how many more people we need to add to the list of suspects.

"Then, we'll review the list, and see where people live. We know that a few guests at the wake came from outside the county, but let's hope that all the immediate suspects are a bit more local.

"By that time, hopefully, we'll be ready to prioritise what to take to the lab. If it's just a few cups and glasses, and maybe food samples, one of you can take them in the car first thing in the morning."

A tap on the door signified the arrival of lunch. Feeke, carrying a coffee pot in one hand, opened the door and led the way. He was closely followed by two maids, bearing two wooden stands. After them came two footmen, each carrying a large mahogany 'butler's tray'.

"George the Third" thought Bryce, admiring the polished wood and the brass-work. The maids unfolded the stands, and the footmen set down the heavy trays. One tray held crockery, glasses, and cutlery. The other held sandwiches, pieces of game pie, seed cake and fruit tartlets. Some oatcakes, with a pat of butter and a generous wedge of Stilton, completed the food selection. Surprisingly, a bottle of white wine was also included, together with a corkscrew.

"Most excellent, Feeke," said Bryce, "and thank you all. I'll thank Mrs Jeff myself later."

Haig had previous experience of seeing what life could be like in an affluent country house, but Kittow's eyes had nearly doubled in circumference as the four servants performed their ritual. Fortunately, nobody had been looking at him.

With Feeke and his staff gone, Kittow gave voice to his astonishment. "Blimey, sir! I've always felt being waited on by Nippies in a Lyons' corner house was rather nice – but this is something else altogether. I could get used to this life, no question. Thanks again for inviting me, sir!"

Bryce laughed. "I suspect that performance was exaggerated from the norm, to make some sort of point. I'm not sure what that might be, but even if the King had been here I doubt if the formality would have been quite so ostentatious. In fact, when coffee was served to the family in the drawing room a little while ago it was a much lower-key performance."

Bryce was quite correct in thinking that a point was being made. Feeke had not forgiven himself for his earlier gaffe regarding the DCI's arrival, and was making amends in the only way he knew.

Bryce picked up the bottle of wine. "Curiouser and curiouser," he said. "This is a fairly exclusive Swiss wine, a Petite Arvine. Considerably better than something I'd expect three humble policemen to be offered at an informal lunch. I've never tried it, but I gather it's pretty well guaranteed to be good.

"Anyway, sorry gentlemen, but we won't be sampling this now. Alcohol is well and good in its place, but halfway through a working day it's not conducive to clear thinking. Tuck into the rest, though."

Bryce mused further as he helped himself to a piece of pie. "I doubt if Lady Ainscough specified the wine, so I wonder if we have the colonel to thank. But he would almost certainly realise that we wouldn't drink at lunchtime. So more likely to be Feeke – and again, I wonder why."

The three men chatted idly on various non-work topics for the next twenty minutes or so. Kittow had been surprised earlier in the day when the DCI used his Christian name, and he had been surprised again a few minutes earlier when the sergeant had told him that, when not actually working, his first name would probably be used again, and that in these circumstances – and these circumstances only – he could omit the usual 'sir' and use 'guv' instead. Nevertheless, Kittow resolved to remain circumspect, just happy to be present, and not wanting to spoil things by speaking out of turn.

When all three were sated, Bryce looked at his watch, a clear signal that they were back at work. "Right, he said. "You might as well get straight off to the PM, Kittow. Best if you fill up the tank while you're out. She'll probably take at least five gallons." He handed over a pound note. "Here, take this, and get a receipt. The police exemption certificate is in the glove box, if the pump attendant should query your allowance.

"The PM is likely to be fairly rudimentary – the doc'll probably just open him up, poke about a bit, bottle some samples, and sew him up again – you'll probably be back here before three thirty, but don't forget the prints."

Bryce turned to Haig when Kittow had gone and admitted:

"I haven't timed this very well. I wonder whether Doreen could be spared now, or whether she is being used at the family lunch."

"Given that it took five to serve the three of us, I imagine that it'd take at least ten to serve five adults and four children," said Haig with a wry smile.

Bryce grinned too. "Tell you what, let's get a bit of fresh air instead. We don't need to bother the staff; we can let ourselves out and walk along as far as the church, or even into the village. We'll aim to get back here by about ten to two, before Isla comes to see us."

The two left the study, crossed the big hall, and found, as expected, that the front door was neither locked nor bolted. Haig lifted the latch, and they exited the house, setting off briskly down the drive.

"Although the design and style of the house is quite different to Broughton Place, sir, and the case is nothing like that one, I still can't help being reminded of it."

"I know what you mean," replied Bryce. "As you say, the cases are totally different. There the owner had been shot dead and the chatelaine was still alive; here the chatelaine is dead – although not, as far as we know, murdered – and the owner is still alive. And the victim isn't even a member of the household at all. I suppose the apparent similarity in our minds is simply that the ambience of a country mansion is common to both."

The two men walked past the church, pausing to examine the lychgate. It was an impressive construction – six massive, and slightly curved oak timbers, standing on low limestone walls at each side and supporting a tiled roof. The view through it, across the graveyard to the old church and even older nearby tower, was beautiful.

However, the lychgate was clearly not of the fifteenth century like the church. For a start it was far larger than a typical example from that period. Bryce surmised that it had been erected in the 1920s, as a memorial to the fallen in the Great War. A closer look confirmed this; on each side ran a stone seat which could double as a coffin rest. Chiselled into the stone on one side was a conventional dedication:

PRO DEO PRO PATRIA

TO REMEMBER THE MEN OF THIS PARISH WHO, AT THE CALL OF DUTY, LAID DOWN THEIR LIVES IN THE GREAT WAR 1914-1919

On the opposite side were inscribed the names of a dozen men, including a Captain John Hardwicke. Haig pointed out the name:

"A brother of the current squire, maybe," he said. "I've never seen a lychgate quite like this before – nor as fine a one."

"Nor have I," replied Bryce. "I believe there were a number built twenty or twenty-five years ago, in some cases replacing old ones that were beyond repair, designed as sort of dual-purpose structures – coffin rest and memorial. This is clearly one of those. Although it's the largest I've seen it isn't at all ostentatious, and indeed I think it's very attractive; but it must have cost a great deal of money. I don't think a whip-round in the parish would have produced enough to make much of a dent in the carpenter's and stonemason's bills!"

The detectives continued along the lane towards the village. It owed its origin, no doubt, to the fact that it was centred on a crossroads. The buildings along the main road were set further back than those on the lesser road, leaving a space in front which, in a larger town, might have been used to hold a market once or twice a week. Bryce wondered if an earlier squire had envisaged a grand future for the village. All the buildings in view, regardless of size and age, were constructed of mostly yellow Cotswold stone, with limestone roof tiles in various shades.

There was a single village shop and post office, and on the opposite side of the street 'The Dog and Partridge Inn', where the Yard men were to stay. The beautifully painted inn sign, swinging gently above the entrance, looked to be fairly new. Mentally reviewing three other pubs he knew with the same name, Bryce recalled that two of the signs showed pointers, and one a retriever. This one had a gorgeous English setter. The partridge, as in the other examples, was unrealistically standing quite happily beside the dog. Bryce didn't know how long the pub had carried its current name, but he thought that had it been 'The Dog and Pheasant' the artist would have had more scope to use colour than for the drab partridge depicted, particularly if a cock – or better still a golden – pheasant had been portrayed.

"Looks a nice enough sort of place, although probably not up to the one in Broughton," remarked Haig. "A pretty village," he continued, "and just a little quieter than Greenford!"

The DCI laughed, and suggested they should make their way back.

CHAPTER 9

On arrival at the manor, Bryce briefly contemplated just opening the door and going in, on the grounds that probably nobody knew they had even left. However, he immediately rejected the idea, and rang the bell instead. This time, a maid came to the door, one of those who had brought in their lunch earlier. With a dainty little bob, she let them in

Bryce contemplated asking if the girl was Doreen, and if so, arranging a time for her interview, but decided against. Maintenance of the hierarchy in a house like this was all-important, particularly amongst the staff. It would be best to arrange the appointment via the butler.

Back in the study, Bryce remembered that his sergeant had left the room to fetch Kittow when Angela had waived her right to be present at the interview with Isla. He explained that the child they were about to see was in fact an honorary niece, and that her mother didn't deem it necessary to be present during the interview. He added that the girl was not in the least shy. The DCI had hardly finished speaking when there was a tap on the door, and it opened to admit a very self-assured Isla.

"Hello, Uncle Philip, she called, running over to Bryce and giving him a hug.

"Mummy and Daddy say you'd like to talk to me about things that happened yesterday. Nobody told me you were here until just now. Are you at work? It's sad about Mr Watson, and of course about Jamjar, too. We don't have to go back to school until Monday," she chattered on.

When he could get a word in, Bryce sat the child down in her grandfather's chair, and introduced his sergeant:

"This is Alex, Isla, he works with me – what we call my right-hand man." Isla immediately stood up again, went around the desk, shook hands politely, and returned to her seat.

She looked at her 'uncle'. "Do you have a left-hand man too?"

Bryce belatedly realised that with a precocious child such as Isla, he might have anticipated such a question. "Oh yes," he replied, "his name is Adam, and he's just gone into town. You may meet him when he gets back later. Now, young lady, you just stay as quiet as you can, apart from answering questions."

Without needing to turn sideways to see Haig's face, he knew that there was a broad grin on it.

"We want to find out how the rector became ill yesterday. We think he must have eaten or drunk something that wasn't good for him."

Seeing Isla was about to interject, he held up a warning hand.

"Your Mother says that you were in the breakfast room yesterday afternoon, and we'd like to talk about that. First, though, just tell us a bit about what went on earlier. When you left the churchyard, and started to come back here, tell us how that was."

"Well, there were lots and lots of people. Grandpa led the way back, with Daddy and Auntie Esther. Then Mummy and Ben and me, and Uncle Henry and Helen and Felix, and Zara and Zena. I didn't really look behind, but I s'pose everyone must have followed."

Isla described how her grandfather had split the family across the various rooms "to look after all our guests".

She described how she and Ben had reached the breakfast room before anyone else, and had each taken a plate and selected some food. Later, they had found a jug of lemonade, and each took a glass of that. The food had been laid out on the buffet sideboards and on one half of the big table, so she and her brother had been able to sit at the other end of the table.

Chattering almost non-stop, Isla explained that after a while, when she got up to talk to people, a man poured a glass of red wine and asked her to take it out to the hall, saying that her grandfather must have something to drink.

"Do you know who the man was, Isla?" asked Bryce.

"I've seen him before, Uncle Philip; but he's not one of Grandpa's tenants – I think he's an old friend, and his name might be Nathan."

"You are doing very well, my dear; everything you say is very helpful. Now, you gave the wine to your grandfather – what did you do next?"

Isla thought for a moment. "I went to the lavatory," she said without embarrassment. "Then I went along to the scullery, 'cos I knew all the staff were in our part of the house and I thought the dogs might be wanting water. But they had plenty, so I just patted them for a bit and then went back to the breakfast room. On the way back I bumped into Helen and Felix, and we talked for a minute.

"In the room, I had another glass of lemonade, and just walked around for a bit talking to people. I like talking," she added unnecessarily.

"Then Grandpa came in, and Ben and I stuck with him for a bit.

"I was by the doors to the parlour, not far from Mummy, when Mr Watson called out to me, and asked me to fetch him a cup of coffee. Black coffee, he wanted.

"I don't really understand coffee, and there wasn't any on the sort of drinks table at that end of the room, but I went to the drinks table at the other end, and I s'pose I must've looked helpless because the man there asked if he could get something for me. I said I needed a coffee, but it had to be black. He said 'Not for you, surely, young miss?' I said it was for Mr Watson, so he picked up a cup and saucer and poured some coffee from a jug thing into the cup. He told me to carry it very carefully because he said the coffee was hot, and we could see it was quite crowded through there in the parlour."

Isla paused for breath, and Bryce took the opportunity to pose a question.

"Do you know who poured the coffee for you?"

"Oh yes, it was Waites, he's one of Grandpa's gamekeepers. He's very good at making funny faces, and I think he'd being doing them for Ben who was standing there when I went for the coffee. But he didn't make any faces while he poured the coffee."

Haig, still very entertained, made a note.

"Now," continued Bryce, "you took the cup from Mr Waites – what did you do next?"

"Oh no. I didn't take the cup at all. I took the saucer really; I didn't touch the cup. And I'm pleased all this is helping you Uncle Philip, but I don't really see how," said Isla.

"Just believe me that it is, my dear – now go on."

"Well, when I took the wine out to Grandpa,

I spilled quite a bit on the way, 'cos the glass was very full to start with and as I walked some kept jumping out, and then I got jostled and lost some more. So I was much more careful with the hot coffee.

"I held the saucer in both hands, and walked slowly towards the parlour. Some people saw I was coming, and made room for me. Others had their backs turned, and I just called out 'excuse me please,' and they moved aside.

"When I got to Mr Watson, he just thanked me and told me to put the coffee down on the table near him. I put it down, talked for a minute to Mr Eccles – he has the Dog and Partridge in the village, and I'm not allowed to go in there yet, but I've met him many times walking his dog when I've been out with Grandpa and Jamjar and our dogs. Then I went to the window and talked to Mrs Wilkin – she was sitting with Mr Eccles' wife, and I'd never met her, so Mrs Wilkin introduced us. Then I was thirsty again and went back to the breakfast room.

"Later, there was a yell, and Mr Watson fell down in pain. Mummy sent Ben and me out of the room, so I didn't see any more. Then this morning they told me that he had died like Jamjar."

She paused again, and this time Haig asked a question.

"As you walked from Mr Waites to the parlour, Isla, did anyone stop you to talk?"

"No, I didn't need to stop at all"

The little nine-year-old looked intelligently

at the two men in turn. "I know what you are thinking," she said. "You think someone put something horrid in the cup as I went along. But they didn't. I was so worried about spilling it that I never took my eyes off it from the moment I took hold of the saucer to the time I put it down on the table in the parlour. I just walked along like this…," She stood up and walked with exaggerated concentration around the room staring down at her hands, held together as if receiving the sacrament.

She returned to her chair, and fell silent, waiting.

Bryce raided an enquiring eyebrow to Haig, who shook his head.

"Thank you, Isla; as I said you have been really helpful. You can run off and do something else now."

"And you can tell your Mummy and Daddy that we were very pleased with the way you told us told us what happened," added Haig.

Isla stood up, shook hands gravely with Sergeant Haig again, gave Bryce another hug, and skipped out.

Haig started to laugh. "Sorry, sir," he spluttered. "What a super wee lassie. As you know, my Rosie will chatter away to people she knows well, but I should think this one could talk for England to a room full of complete strangers. Also, and I hope it won't be necessary, I doubt if being in the witness box would faze her – and I bet she'd be really convincing too.

"Anyway, her evidence seems very clear. If it was the coffee at all, either Waites slipped the poison into the cup, or it was done after the coffee arrived on the table in the parlour."

"Agreed. But here's another thought. Clearly both Waites and Isla handled the cup. Or, as Isla pedantically explained, the saucer. And assuming, as you say, that the cup was the vehicle for the strychnine, Watson must have picked it up too. But there would almost certainly be no need for the poisoner to touch the cup at all, so fingerprints are unlikely to help us."

Not for the first time in their partnership, the two men sat silently, wishing things were clearer. Eventually, Bryce rose and pressed the bell.

Feeke himself answered. "You rang, sir?" the butler enquired.

"Yes, thank you, Feeke. If it's convenient, I wonder if you can spare Doreen for a short while? As you know, she was near to the rector when he was taken ill, and she may have seen something relevant."

"Certainly, sir," replied the butler, appreciating the chief inspector's knowledge of, and also respect for, protocol. "She's just having a cup of tea in the servants' hall. I'll have her come along here directly."

The butler bowed, and withdrew. Shortly afterwards there was a tap on the door, and in response to Bryce's "come in" a maid entered the room. The DCI looked at her, noting that she wasn't the one who had come to the front door, but had been in the contingent who brought the lunch. Doreen looked to be about twenty, attractive without being beautiful, wearing a neat uniform and with her black hair bunched under a little white cap. She waited expectantly, and seemed nervous.

Bryce and Haig stood up, and Bryce shook the girl's hand. The sergeant had seen him behave with impeccable politeness to servant witnesses before, and so almost expected his chief's action, but Doreen was clearly surprised, and hesitated for a second before taking his offered hand.

"This is very informal," said Bryce. "Take a seat here, please." He indicated one of the chairs, and this time sat in the colonel's chair himself, with Haig seated on the other side. Both could now observe the witness.

"Doreen, I want you to forget who you are and what your job is here. During the wake, you were just a guest at the wake, and that is your role again now."

The girl nodded.

"Now it was very unpleasant, especially for you, yesterday, and I'm sorry to have to make you go through it again. But I imagine that you've been told that the rector died through being poisoned, and you'll understand that we want to find out who was responsible. I need hardly say that nobody is suggesting that you had anything to do with it – but it is possible that you might have seen something which might help us."

"I understand, sir," replied the maid in a delightful Oxfordshire accent. "I didn't really know Mr Watson, not being a church sort of person, but murder is horrid, and I'd like to help you find who killed him. I don't think I know anything though," she added.

"Perhaps not, but let's go through the events and see.

"Start by telling us your full name, and then just explain how you and everyone else came into the house, and how it was that you were standing where you were."

"I'm Doreen Elsie Rolfe. Well, sir, when the funeral service was finished, it had been agreed that we house staff would come straight back to the house to get things ready, and not stay for the burial. Me, Mr Feeke, and Mrs Walters and the others hurried back here. Mrs Walters had already ordered everything and decided where things would go, and Cook and the girls in the kitchen had done all the food and covered it up ready. All we had to do was carry everything through to the breakfast room and the dining room. Didn't take but twenty minutes. Cook made great urns of tea and coffee at the last minute, and Mr Feeke had already decanted a lot of red wine. There was white wine and sherry as well, and plenty of pop for the children and any teetotallers.

"Anyway, when everything was set out

proper, sir, Mr Feeke told us that the colonel wanted us to be ordinary guests as far as possible, although to start with he wanted someone to be on the door of some of the rooms to guide the visitors. But I wasn't given a job, so when my fiancé – he's a gardener here – arrived, we went into the breakfast room. We were about the first there, I think, apart from Mrs Angela and her children. Very nice she was, gave us plates, told us to choose lots of food, and chatted to us before more people came in.

"Well, as a few more people come in we sort of moved on into the parlour. One or two others that I knew – Marcus Eccles and his wife Edith, and Adelaide Wilkin, come in about the same time. The two ladies went straight away to sit in the comfy chairs, and Tony and me just talked to Mr Eccles. He's a right laugh, he is, sir. There was others what I only knew by sight, like Mr Dauntsey and Mr McKay, they're regular visitors to the house but I never talked with them before yesterday.

"There was also an elderly, very pleasant gentleman, named Hicks. He's a retired major and been here before. He told us that he'd known the colonel for fifty years, and he said that was longer than anyone else could boast.

"Oh, and there was Silas Anderson, one of the farmers, I'd spoken to him once or twice before.

"Then the rector, he come in and stood up our end of the parlour. And another man, much younger, in a dog collar too – I didn't catch his name and nobody else seemed to know him either.

"The rector didn't speak to me 'cept once, but I must say that the gentlemen like Mr McKay and the major were very nice and polite to people like me and Tony."

"I'm pleased to hear it, Doreen," said Bryce. "They were quite right to do that – you were guests at Mrs Hardwicke's wake, exactly the same as they were."

"Oh, yes, and the colonel joined us for a few minutes at one point, sir. He knew about me and Tony, and congratulated us. He talked about Mrs Beth's will, and her not having much money of her own. But he didn't stay long."

"What you've told us ties in exactly with Mrs Angela's plan which she drew for us, and it's always nice to get two or more people giving the same picture.

"Now, let's see if you can help us a bit more. When the rector came in, was he already carrying a plate of food?"

"Yes, I'm almost certain. Oh yes, and he put the plate down on the table and started talking. He didn't have a drink, though, and a few minutes later he told me to fetch him a glass of red wine from the breakfast room. I got the impression some of the others felt he should have gone himself, but I went just the same. I didn't really feel I could say no. The very tall man standing by the drinks table – I heard someone call him 'Sir Nathan' – asked if he could help. He poured the wine for me. I took it back to the parlour, and the rector just pointed where I should put it down on the table. So I did, and he went on talking."

Doreen paused, and looked at the officers to see whether she should continue.

"Carry on please, Doreen, you're doing very well," said Bryce.

"Well, I think the rector must have drunk the wine, because later he called across to Miss Isla – she's Mr Miles' and Mrs Angela's daughter – and asked her to bring him some coffee. And she did, and put it down on the table just as I did. Then she wandered off to talk to other people. Very chatty little girl is Miss Isla; not even a little bit backward in coming forward, as my Mum would say!"

Doreen paused, seemingly to prepare herself for talking about the unpleasantness which followed.

"Well, sir, the rector, he'd eaten his food, and drunk his wine and coffee. I thought he might ask me to bring him something more, as I was nearer the breakfast room than anyone else around. But suddenly he seemed to turn a funny colour and started groaning and clutching himself. Then he fell to the floor, and I let out a scream – I just couldn't help it, sir. Then it got even worse, because he started sort of kicking and jerking around as he lay there."

Doreen visibly paled as she remembered the detail of the incident. Bryce locked his grey eyes on hers, said nothing, and silently encouraged her to complete her recount.

"Someone went for Dr Ford, and even before he come the gents at the drinks table shooed us out of the parlour, through the breakfast room, and into the corridor.

"Tony and me, we was in the hall, and then a bit later we saw the ambulance come. We thought it was just his appendix or something, and it was a real shock when Sergeant Jarvis come, and we heard the rector'd died."

"Thank you, Doreen, that's all been very helpful," Bryce assured the girl, "but I do have some questions.

"When you went for the wine, and the gentleman poured it for you, did he know for whom you wanted it, or did you let him assume it was for you?"

"Oh, I told him it was for the rector, and the man said something like 'a nice dose of Burgundy'll bring the roses to his pale cheeks'."

"And did you watch him actually pour the wine?"

"Yes, sir, and then I took it back to the parlour, like I said."

Doreen was not demonstrating the acuity that the far younger Isla had shown earlier.

"Yes, I see," said Bryce. He decided that he would have to spell things out. "From the time Sir Nathan picked up the empty glass, to the time you set it down on the parlour table, could anyone have put anything in it that shouldn't be there?"

"I don't see how, sir. Oh, Lord, you mean

someone poisoned the wine!"

"It's just a possibility, Doreen, that's all. It's not even quite certain what caused his death yet, although it seems likely that he ate or drank something. At this stage we're just looking at everything."

"I see, sir," said Doreen falteringly, looking unsure and extremely apprehensive. After taking a few seconds to assimilate the possibility that she had carried the fatal beverage to the rector, she suddenly blurted:

"The cup of coffee, sir, it might have been that, not my wine!"

"Yes, that's right, Doreen; there's no suggestion this has anything to do with you or the wine. We knew about the coffee, and we've had a chat with Miss Isla just as we are doing with you."

Bryce glanced at Haig, "I think the sergeant has a couple of questions before you go."

"Yes, sir, thank you. Doreen, you've told us about the wine and the coffee. Did you see anyone else, at any time, bring the rector any more food or drink?"

"No, sir; I was standing close by him from the time he came into the parlour, and I'm sure nobody brought him anything else."

"Good. Now, you told us that the rector probably put his plate down on the table when he first came into the parlour. There were several people standing around nearby, and you've told us who they were. Did you see anyone touching that plate – apart from the rector himself, of course? Pinching one of his sandwiches, for instance?"

Doreen took the question literally. "Who would want to steal his sandwiches?" she asked. "It was only a few yards' walk to the breakfast room table and buffet."

Haig, who was not naturally patient, had learned something of the art from his boss. "No, of course not," he laughed. "But with the drink – could someone have added anything while the wine glass or coffee cup stood on the table?"

The maid appeared to give this more specific question a great deal of thought. Eventually, she said:

"I don't know. You see where I stood, and I didn't move very much, there were other people sort of blocking my view of the bit of the table nearest to the rector. Himself, for a start, and he was a big man. Then there were people sort of behind him as well."

"Yes, we can see that, Doreen," said Bryce. "I think it might be helpful if you just draw us a little plan, just like Mrs Angela has done for us." Angela's plan was face-down on the table, and Bryce pulled it in front of him and took out a pencil. "Look, I'll just draw the table, which was against the wall, blocking the door. Can you please put a little blob to show the rough position of a person, and then put a number beside it – one to nine or whatever. Then you can tell us who the numbers represent – number one for the rector, for example."

"I'll do my best, sir," replied the girl. "Of course, people might have moved around in the group a little bit, but once we were all there I don't think anyone else came or went, apart from when the colonel came, and Miss Isla with the coffee."

She looked at the paper, hesitated, and slowly added a number of dots around the short and long side of the table. She then wrote a number beside each dot.

"Shall I write the names with their numbers underneath?" She asked, demonstrating intelligence for the first time.

"Aye, good idea," said Haig.

Two minutes later, the girl pushed the plan back to the DCI. He and Haig looked at it. Without turning the paper over, they could see that essentially it showed the same people in roughly the same positions as in Angela's sketch.

"That's excellent, Doreen," said Haig. "Just one last question from me, and I'm sure you're expecting it:

"Can you think of any reason for someone to dislike the rector?"

The maid looked flustered. "Nobody would want to kill him, surely?" she stammered.

"Somebody did," said Bryce with gentle emphasis. "But you haven't answered the sergeant's question. Who do you know who had a dislike of Simeon Watson, or who might have had some sort of disagreement with him?"

Doreen looked as though she wasn't going to

reply, but as both officers continued to gaze at her expectantly, she said:

"It's gossip, really – only what I've heard, and I'm not saying any of it's right or wrong! It's said that the rector complained to Mr Eccles about noise after closing time, and also about drinking after hours. I heard as well that he threatened to report Mr Eccles to the licensing justices, or some such."

"That's better, Doreen, but I think you still have a wee bit more information for us," said Haig.

After another silence, again with the girl seeming to have a mental struggle, she at last said:

"Oh dear, I'm sure I shouldn't say this, and please don't tell anyone that I did, but I think the rector had an affair with Vicky Anderson – she's married to Silas. I don't know anyone else who might have hated the rector, I really don't."

"Thank you, Doreen," said Bryce. Rest assured that nobody will ever learn that you have given us those bits of information. And of course they – and the wine and the coffee – might not be significant in this case anyway. Off you go now."

CHAPTER 10

When the door closed behind her, the two men relaxed.

"Very well done, sergeant; you obviously thought, as did I, that she was hiding at least one more snippet of gossip, and you extracted that nicely. So, what can we deduce from the three interviews so far?"

Internally rejoicing at the praise, Haig gave his thoughts:

"First, all three pretty much agree on who stood where, and how the food and drink moved around, so that's good. In my opinion, sir, unless we hear that it's not strychnine after all, we should concentrate on the wine and the coffee."

"Agreed," said Bryce; "go on."

"I'm still not convinced that Doreen has told us everything she knows or suspects," said Haig.

"But taking her evidence as it stands, if the poison was in the wine, then until she put the glass down on the table only she or the general had contact with it.

"Much the same with the coffee; it's impossible to believe that Isla did it, and her evidence about watching the cup all the way convinced me. So again, until the coffee cup was put down, only Waites could have interfered with it.

"Then, looking at who could have tampered with either wine or coffee, we have the same set of suspects. Leaving aside the rector, we have Doreen's fiancé Bixby; Anderson; Eccles; the dog-collared chap Edwards; McKay; Hicks; Dauntsey. Plus Doreen herself, although if she was going to do it one would think it would be before she put the glass down.

"Of those, we hear that Eccles has reason to dislike the victim, as does Anderson. We've had this before, though – motives that don't really look strong enough to be a reason for murder. Although if the facts about Mrs Anderson are correct, Anderson's motive would rank ahead of Eccles' motive, in my book.

"Overall, sir, I think that it's most likely the tampering was done at the table."

"Good summary, Haig. Like you, I'm not convinced that Doreen has told us everything she knows. In any case, the colonel admitted to me earlier that he himself didn't always see eye-to-eye with the rector, and you heard Miss Lacon allude to 'spats' with 'several' locals. To me, 'several' means more than just Anderson and Eccles, so we'll have to ask the colonel. It's also possible that we may be able to glean some gossip from other servants.

"I don't know about you, but I'm parched again. I think a cup of tea is needed." Haig agreed, and being nearest to the button, rang the bell.

Feeke arrived, and was followed into the room by Kittow.

"Ah, Feeke. Find the colonel and present my compliments, please. Ask him if it's convenient to have the chat we talked about earlier. If it is, then perhaps we could have tea for four – if he isn't available then tea for three, please." ordered Bryce.

"Also, see if you can find Mr Miles or Mrs Angela, and ask if young Master Ben could come along and see us."

"Very good, sir, I'll put all that in hand." The butler bowed, and withdrew.

"I suppose since we've already seen Isla, the other children might feel left out, so we may need to invite Helen and Felix later. However, they don't seem to have been in the relevant rooms at all." Turning to Kittow he said:

"Take a seat and tell us how you got on."

The DC took his pocketbook out of his jacket in readiness and said, "It wasn't too bad, sir. Worst thing was the horrible chemical smell; formaldehyde, the doc said it was. Anyway, he's a nice chap, kept up a running commentary the whole time, saying what he was doing. As you said, he put a lot of stuff in jars – they're all going off for analysis, and they have local facilities for that. He said the results will be back by tomorrow, and that he's ninety-nine percent certain it's strychnine."

Kittow consulted his pocketbook. "A massive dose, he says, as the time from first symptoms to death was so short. A couple of grains, he says it could be.

"Oh, and the Coroner's Officer was there. He said that the brother had been in to make a formal identification. He also said that the Coroner will wait for the analysis, and then convene an inquest, probably for the day after tomorrow, sir. He'll let you know as soon as it's decided.

"And I took the deceased's prints, sir."

"Good. Well, I can't say that we've made much progress since you left." Bryce relayed his conversation with Haig and added:

"We think the strychnine was most likely in the coffee or the red wine. If we accept for the moment that it wasn't put in by the general who poured the wine, or the gamekeeper who poured the coffee, then the microscope needs to be focused on the people standing around Watson. We know from the two drawings done that there were eight people standing close to the victim.

"Of those, so far we've only seen Doreen. One final fact for us to consider. At least two of these people had some reason to dislike the victim. But we believe it's probable there were others."

A tap at the door brought Feeke back into the room.

"Beg pardon sir, but when I spoke to Mrs

Angela about Ben, Miss Helen and Master Felix were also in the room, and asked if they could come too. Lady Ainscough said that it was up to you, sir, but that if you agreed you were to 'turf them out' after five minutes. And Miss Isla wanted a second 'turn', but Mrs Angela said she'd had more than her fair share. She did, however, promise the young lady that you'd come along in the Christmas holidays and take her to the pantomime."

Haig stifled a snort. Clearly Isla's mother was also 'not backward in coming forward', as Doreen's mum might say.

"The children are all outside, sir. As there aren't many chairs the colonel says he'll give you a few minutes before he comes in."

"Very well, Feeke; show them in, if you please."

Feeke opened the door again, and stood aside as three children came in – one running, and two more slowly. Ben, who knew Bryce as well as his sister did, immediately climbed up on Bryce's knee. Helen and Felix, who had not met him before, were more reserved, and stood quietly while he explained who he was.

Bryce introduced the children to his subordinates. Helen, like her cousin earlier, gravely shook hands with Haig and also Kittow.

"Which one is your 'left-hand man', Uncle Philip?" enquired Ben, who had evidently been briefed by his sister.

Bryce pointed to Kittow, and then of course

had to explain to the DC what had occurred earlier in the afternoon.

"Helen, Felix, I'm sorry we don't have enough chairs, but perhaps you could perch on the window seat.

"You all know that, quite apart from the sadness about your grandma, the rector was taken ill and died. You also know that I'm a detective, and it's my job to find out what happened.

"I need to ask Ben a couple of questions, and then any of you can tell us anything you think we might not know.

"Now, Ben, think about yesterday afternoon, when you were in the breakfast room. I believe Mr Waites was making funny faces for you?"

"Oh yes. He's jolly good at those!" said the boy enthusiastically, making a few pretty tame faces himself a few inches from Bryce's nose. "He's shown me before, but he told me yesterday that he has 'increased his reppycha' and had some new ones to show me."

The tea arrived at this point, and Bryce allowed the boy to carry on with his little display until the maids had left.

"Now, Ben, while you were with Mr Waites, did Isla come and join you?"

"Yes, that's right, Uncle Philip. She wanted a drink to take to the rector. Waites poured coffee into a cup and said it was very hot, and told Isla to be careful." Ben leaned forward at this point and confided "I've never drunk coffee myself, but I think it smells jolly nice."

"Good," said Bryce. "Did you watch as Waites was pouring the coffee?"

"Oh yes; I hoped he'd make some more faces. But he didn't. Not 'til after Isla had gone."

"And did you watch your sister as she went back to the parlour?"

The boy's face showed astonishment at the question. "No, I didn't, Uncle. Should I have done?"

Bryce laughed. "No," he said, "there was no need for you to do that. You've been very helpful, Ben, thank you."

He turned to the boy's cousins. "Helen, Felix, I understand from your Aunt Angela that you weren't in the breakfast room and parlour at all. Is that right?"

"Yes," replied Helen. "After we got our food from the dining room we were with Mummy and Daddy in the drawing room to begin with, and then later we went into the hall and talked to guests. Felix is a bit shy, so I did most of the talking. I took sandwiches to Grandfather quite early on when he was still in the hall. Later, we sat with the other children and a terribly nice old lady who showed us her lace shawl and told us how she'd made it with bobbins and thread."

"Good, that's all clear, Helen, thanks. Now, did any of you see anything before the rector was taken away to hospital that you thought seemed a bit unusual?"

The three children looked at each other.

Once again Helen spoke for the trio.

"It's difficult to answer that. None of us had ever been to a funeral before, or a wake. So, for me anyway, everything seemed very strange." Both boys nodded.

"But if you mean did we see anyone doing anything really suspicious, well I didn't – and if Felix or Ben had I'm sure they'd have shared it by now."

More nodding from the boys confirmed this.

"Fair enough, Helen, you've explained that very well. Right, thank you all very much. You can run along now."

He set Ben down off his knee and tousled his head, only then noticing that Colonel Hardwicke had entered the room silently, and was standing by the door. All three children gave him a hug as they went out. The men stood up.

"Hello, colonel, I didn't see you come in. May I offer you a cup of tea in your own house?"

Hardwicke laughed, remembering how his friends had turned him into a guest the day before. "Yes please," he said. "Milk but no sugar."

Kittow poured the extra cup, and as he had been sitting in the colonel's chair, took his own cup over to the window seat.

"I bring you news of Sergeant Jarvis," said Hardwicke. He's just telephoned to say that he has 'scrounged a car', as he thought that might make him more useful to you. He asked if he should bring the car when he returns at four o'clock. I told him I'd pass the message on and that you would ring him back."

"Thank you, colonel," said the DCI, very pleased with the prospect of an additional vehicle. He turned to Kittow and gave instructions:

"Use the telephone in the hall to ring Jarvis and thank him on my behalf. Tell him the car will be very welcome tomorrow, but that I don't have an immediate task for him today, so he's to carry on with his usual duties. He should pick me up at the Dog and Partridge at eight thirty in the morning."

CHAPTER 11

Hardwicke regarded the chief inspector:

"As you heard earlier, I didn't know that you are a friend of Miles and Angela and the children. Isla was full of how she'd helped you solve the murder, and I could see what Ben thought of you just now. I'll say again; please visit one day, in less stressful times, of course, when the children are also here.

"But assuming that Isla exaggerated, Bryce, I imagine that you have more questions to ask me. I'm under no illusions about being a suspect."

"Alas, yes, I'm afraid Isla was being a tad optimistic, colonel. We are moving along, but there's no breakthrough yet.

"Anyway, there are a few questions for you. First, I assume there is a rectory – did the rector live by himself?"

"Yes, there is a rectory – damn great mid-nineteenth century monstrosity. Suited a rector with a wife, eight children, and a brace of staff for each of them. As for living alone, it depends on your definition, I suppose. Watson wasn't married, but he kept a cook/housekeeper and a maid-of-all-work, both of whom lived in. With such a limited staff I assume much of the house is shut off. I haven't been in it for years because he didn't entertain; although I can tell you the living here is well remunerated thanks to an unusual endowment which is outside the reach of the Church authorities. So he could have afforded to entertain, if he had wanted to do so.

"Probably helpful if I also tell you that the rectory here is part of the estate, and nothing to do with the Church. Another unusual arrangement. With Watson gone, everything is down to me – so you won't need a warrant or anything, Bryce. I'll call and inform Mrs Ellis that you'll be coming, if you like."

"Very helpful, colonel – one or more of us will go around as soon as we've finished talking to you," said Bryce.

"I think I told you earlier that I invited Watson to my table every so often. It was really a matter of respect for his position – and he only ever came if we had other guests. He held boringly rigid views on everything under the sun, and had little patience for anyone who held contrary opinions. Beth and I preferred to have a few other people around our table when he came, rather than endure him on our own!"

"I see; very clear, thank you," said Bryce.

"Apparently his brother has been to identify the body – do you know him?"

"Met him a couple of times. Same type of chap, unfortunately, although not a priest. I don't think they were close.

"Incidentally, you'll want to know about Watson's will. I've no idea of the contents, of course – but I know that Travis McKay, my solicitor, prepared one for him."

The colonel sat back in his chair and drank some tea before continuing. "I only know about that because McKay, in a rare moment of indiscretion, told me that Watson, despite reminders, had never paid his bill for preparing it. I believe you barristers aren't allowed to sue for your fees, but as a solicitor McKay could have done. Didn't want the unwelcome publicity perhaps. But I really can't see McKay murdering him over that; I'm only adding it in to help you build a picture of Watson.

Bryce nodded. "I understand that you yourself went into the parlour at one point, and spoke to the people in the rector's group. We've heard from other witnesses, and nobody saw anything suspicious. We can assume that if you'd seen anyone acting suspiciously you'd have said so already. But while you were present was there any suggestion of unpleasantness of any sort?"

"Nothing like that at all. I doubt I was there for much above five minutes, but it all seemed very normal to me. I was a bit distracted, of course, so it's possible there was some undercurrent that I didn't pick up."

The colonel looked up at the ceiling and retraced yesterday's conversations.

"I congratulated Bixby and Doreen, and I promised to make an early appointment with Dauntsey to discuss estate business. I explained that there wasn't going to be a formal reading of Beth's will. That was about it. I didn't speak directly to Watson, nor to the others. And yes, of course I understand that I must be high up on your list of suspects, but I can assure you that I haven't killed anyone since 1917."

"We had already heard that the rector wasn't universally popular," said Bryce. "You'll appreciate, of course, that finding a motive is a key component in any criminal case. Is there anything else you know of which could cause someone else to detest the man – however unlikely it might be that murder would ensue?"

"Yes, I understand. It's very difficult. '*Nil nisi bonum*' and all that. On the other hand, we must find the culprit. Anyway, as I've already made one criticism, I suppose it would be absurd to hold back now. I'll tell you what else I know. Or rather, as all of this is hearsay, what I've been told."

The colonel took some more tea to lubricate his vocal cords. "Unless you say otherwise, I'll limit my reports – or gossip – to people who were standing with Watson yesterday.

"First, there was Eccles, the landlord of the

local. Apparently, Watson had really taken agin him – threatened to have his licence revoked. I drop in for the occasional pint, and I don't have anything against Eccles – he's not the sort of person who hangs around trying to ingratiate himself with the squire. Serves the drink and then moves away, unless you choose to engage him in conversation. I don't know what beef Watson had – and although Eccles is my tenant I really didn't want to get involved. I'd just say two things:

"If he did lose his licence he'd have been out of work, and after a time I'd inevitably have had to evict him and find another publican, so he'd lose his home as well.

"On the other hand, in the unlikely event that he decided to kill Watson, surely he could find a far more suitable venue in which to do it – and an easier way?

"The second piece of gossip is this: it seems Watson seriously upset Doreen, one of my maids. I gather you've talked to her, so she has probably mentioned this?"

Bryce shook his head and then shot a raised eyebrows glance at Haig. It seemed they were about to hear the information that they both believed Doreen was withholding.

"Last week, Beth found her crying and asked what the trouble was. Doreen told her that she and Bixby had just been to see Watson about getting married. He flatly refused to allow them to marry in the church – on the grounds, apparently, that neither of them was a regular churchgoer. Beth's death the next day meant that I haven't followed this up, although if Watson had dug his heels in, I wouldn't have had the power to overrule him. I should still have said my piece on the matter, though."

"I see," said Bryce. "It doesn't really seem much of a reason to kill anyone, unless Bixby is a particularly short-tempered individual?"

"No," said Hardwicke firmly, "I've never seen any sign of that. A quiet, polite young man. And I know it's always said that poison is a woman's weapon, but Doreen is also a quiet, self-effacing girl – and not the sharpest tool in the box, either."

"Quite so. It's all grist to the mill, colonel, so please carry on."

Hardwicke hesitated, a frown appearing on his forehead. "Now I'm starting to talk about these things, I'm realising for the first time how they have mounted up. Frankly, it's all pretty awful!

"This next rumour only reached me a couple of days ago, and again I haven't had the opportunity to enquire further. I hear that Victoria Anderson, wife of one of the tenant farmers, has been having an affair with Watson. Anderson is a good man. He runs the farm well, and is a first-class shot. He's a handsome chap, about forty, I suppose. Vicky is a few years younger, and good-looking, in her own way. I'd describe Watson as a big ugly man, and he must have been twenty years her senior. If the rumour is true, there's absolutely no accounting for taste is all I can say about it."

Haig, who had been jotting down the main points during the colonel's interview, now raised his head:

"Do you know if Mr Anderson is aware of the liaison, sir?"

"Good question, sergeant; I have no idea of the answer. But even if he did know, I can't believe he'd commit murder – although he's certainly not the sort of man who puts up with any nonsense from anyone. However, I suppose that this bit of tittle-tattle, if true, does provide a rather stronger motive than the other rumours.

"The final bit of gossip, gentlemen, concerns my land agent, James Dauntsey. Another competent chap; came here a few months after the end of the war. I knew his father slightly – from a cadet branch of a notable family himself – when he was agent to Lord Shawbourne on the other side of the county, back in the thirties.

"I have absolutely no complaint against Dauntsey. Although he never attends church, I certainly don't hold that against him. Off the record, I really only attend myself because it's a sort of duty. Now Beth has gone, there won't be anyone to push me into going. Anyway, apparently Watson recently discovered that Dauntsey isn't just a non-attender, but is an avowed atheist. He came to the house last week, and told me that as he had failed to persuade Dauntsey to 'find God', I should dismiss him."

The colonel shook his head at the memory of the distasteful conversation. "We have freedom of religion in this country, I told him, including the right to practise no religion, and that he was utterly ridiculous in calling upon me to sack the best agent I'm likely to find. He got quite heated at my refusal, and we actually exchanged a few sharp words. That's happened before, though, but we always got back on peaceful terms soon enough.

"Once again, I haven't had a chance to talk to Dauntsey about this, so he probably doesn't know that I sent Watson packing. I was rather surprised to see the two of them were apparently standing in close proximity for some time yesterday."

The colonel came to a halt. "Hope that lot of hearsay proves helpful, Bryce. Not at all sure that it will, though. You'll talk to Mrs Ellis at the rectory, no doubt, and the maid too – I don't know her name. If you want any more background, you might try Thompson, the churchwarden – he's worked with Watson for years.

"I would suggest Feeke, but although I don't doubt he knows everything that goes on in the parish. He's as tight as an oyster, and even I wouldn't be able to extract any pearls – but I certainly wish you joy if you want to try yourself! The next best is Waites, my gamekeeper. He was here yesterday too, and you may already be thinking of talking to him. A real character, and a garrulous soul."

Hardwicke sat back and finished his tea.

Bryce thought he looked weary and run down.

"Something in all that may well prove crucial, colonel. In any case, as you point out, it helps build a picture for us. Only one more thing:

"As yet I have no idea how many of your guests we'll need to interview. Initially, we're limiting the list to those who were in the group around the rector in the time before he was taken ill, plus those – like you and Isla – who moved in and out of that group at some time.

"Of the nine or ten people, most appear to be local, but we don't know about Major Hicks and Mr Edwards. Do you have addresses for them?"

"I can find Edwards' details again easily enough, I'm sure. Esther trawled through Beth's desk to find her address-cum-telephone book when she was informing people of the arrangements, so Edward's contact details must be in there. I'll dig it out and let you have it.

"Meantime, I can tell you he has a curacy, somewhere in the east end of London, I think. Can't abide the man, myself. Whereas Watson relished disagreeing with someone, Edwards is the complete opposite – agrees with whatever you say. I actually think that's worse. He's also an awful snob. God knows how he gets on with the poor parishioners of Plaistow, or wherever it is.

"As for Hicks and all the others in that group, their details are all in my address book, right here." Hardwicke opened his desk drawer and removed a thick leather-bound volume with a brass clasp and corners. Passing it to Bryce, he stood up, ready to leave.

"That's fine, thank you, colonel. And thank you again for the use of this room – and of course for the food and drink which we've enjoyed."

Kittow, who had unobtrusively slipped back into the room after making his telephone call, stood and opened the study door for the colonel.

Bryce turned to his colleagues and asked, "Either of you voting for our host as the murderer?"

Haig and Kittow shook their heads.

"No, I don't think so either," agreed the DCI. "It's always risky, mentally eliminating suspects at an early stage. It's even worse to discard evidence before it's been properly evaluated. However, in a situation where we have too many suspects and too much evidence, we must make some measured assumptions.

"Now is a good time for a thorough exchange of views, before I decide how to move things forwards." Bryce, who had already had such an exchange with Haig, was keen to hear Kittow's assessment of the case. He looked at his junior man, "I've heard the sergeant's views, so you have a go, constable."

Kittow moistened his lips. His role so far had been to carry the murder bag, and to watch and listen as Haig decided how to set up his camera angles. Like the car journey to Mistram, everything had been very 'back seat' for him. He had, however, given almost non-stop thought to the mechanics of how the rector's assailant had accomplished the deed. He spoke his mind:

"If we look at the strychnine being in the food, sir, then my first thought was a member of staff or family must be responsible." He rushed on eagerly, "I can see a lot of ways how staff might do it – either in the kitchen; or while bringing the food up to the tables. Or even later, between when the food was already put out and the guests hadn't arrived. Same goes for the family, really.

"But then I run into problems, sir. First of all, everyone helped themselves. So how could anyone be sure the rector would take what they wanted him to?"

Having undermined his own theory, Kittow rushed on, "I can actually get around that a little bit, though, by thinking instead that the poisoned food wouldn't be on a serving plate – far too risky that someone else would pick it up – and that somehow, it had to be put directly onto the rector's plate."

"Aye," said Haig, "in a busy room, with people moving their plates on and off the same table, I don't find that idea impossible to accept."

Encouraged by the smile he could now see appearing on the DCI's face, Kittow pressed on again, "Of course if that's how it was done, sir, then it doesn't have to be staff or family who put the food on the rector's plate. It could have been any of the others around him. Just slip the food out of a pocket and onto his plate."

Kittow had never voiced his own thoughts at such length before. His superiors looked pleased with him, and he wondered if he had reached a 'quit while you're ahead moment'. However, noticing the silence from his DCI and sergeant, he felt he was being encouraged to continue.

"The harder parts for me, sir, are accepting that the rector wouldn't look down on his plate of food, that he's just collected for himself, and see something that he either hadn't chosen – or maybe didn't even like and would never have chosen. Also, someone carrying a sandwich around in their pocket for any length of time would probably produce such a fluff-covered curled up offering that the rector wouldn't have touched it anyway. And then there's the food – I don't know what sort of foodstuffs would actually mask strychnine." Kittow rushed to his conclusion, "That's why I don't think it was the food at all, sir. I think the rector was slipped a deadly Mickey Finn in a drink."

"Well done, Kittow," said Bryce warmly. "I don't disagree with anything you've said, or your reasoning, which is much the same as the sergeant's earlier. My bet is also on one of the drinks being tampered with, and that our chief suspects are those who stood with the rector, plus perhaps Waites and Vickery who poured the coffee and wine. It's not unprecedented to have that number of suspects, but the proportion of them with reason to detest the victim – at least six out of the eight – is certainly higher than usual.

"How have you got on with isolating the cups and glasses, Kittow?"

"Just about done, sir. I've only sorted and labelled those on the main parlour table, as you said. Plus the glass under the table. I've not touched the plates or the food."

"Good. Don't bother with the food. These are the next few tasks: we'll go to the parlour now, and finish bagging up the glasses and cups. Tomorrow morning, I want you two to take them to Hendon. It's a far smaller load than we'd anticipated, so it will all easily fit into the car," said Bryce, pleased that the need to organise a van had been avoided.

"Then, as you're in London, go and find this priest chap, Edwards; get his interview out of the way. While you're doing that, I'll see all the more local people: Messrs Dauntsey, McKay, Bixby, and Hicks – and I'll see Eccles tomorrow as well, if we don't get a chance to chat to him this evening.

"I'm making another big decision. After we've got the glasses and so on in the car, I propose to tell the staff that they can clear the two rooms, and then hand them back to the family. Comments?"

"I'd say it's the most practicable decision, sir," said Haig. Kittow nodded.

"Okay, well the last thing today will be to go along to the rectory. We'll take a look at whatever papers we can find to see if there's anything which might shed some light. We'll also interview the two women, although it's possible all we'll get there is a bit more colour to add to the picture the colonel painted.

"After that, it'll certainly be time for some food and bed."

The three men made their way to the parlour, and re-commenced the task of getting the samples ready for transporting. That done, Bryce took one last look around both rooms, and then pressed the breakfast room bell.

When Feeke responded, Bryce explained that the breakfast room and parlour could now be cleared whenever convenient, and when that was done the colonel should be informed that the rooms were once again available for use.

Hardwicke looked into the breakfast room at this point, and heard what the DCI had said.

"Thanks for that, Bryce. I didn't expect to get the rooms back that quickly. It's the parlour I'm really looking forward to having. Anyway, I've brought the addresses you wanted – telephone numbers too. I've also told Mrs Ellis you'll be coming."

Bryce took the list, and thanked him.

"We're all going to the rectory now, colonel, and then to the inn for the night. I'll be back here sometime in the morning."

CHAPTER 12

The three officers went out to the car.

"The rectory is just behind the church," said Bryce. "It's walking distance, but we'd have to come back here to get the car anyway, as our bags are in it. It's easiest to take it now. You drive again, Kittow."

Minutes later, the car drew up in front of the rectory. All three men thought how accurate the colonel's description had been. A three-storey building, which for some reason had been constructed in grey granite instead of the local stone. It was indeed a 'monstrosity', but even if most of the property was unoccupied, someone was at least making an effort to care for it, with the front garden tended, and the windows clean.

The three detectives approached the front door and Haig knocked, using what was evidently the original brass knocker. This clearly received a regular polishing.

The door was opened by a sad-looking

woman in her early sixties. A shapeless grey dress hung loosely over her washboard figure, her thinning white hair tightly pulled back in an unflattering knot at the back of her head.

"You'll be the police," she said glumly. "Squire said to expect you. Come in.

"You'd better come straight through to the rector's study, sir; I expect you'll want to look through his things. Squire said you'd want to talk to Alice and me, too."

"Yes, thank you Mrs Ellis, that's right. I'm Chief Inspector Bryce, and this is Sergeant Haig and Constable Kittow."

The woman took them into a small room, which contained little but a big desk, a bookcase, two upright chairs and one armchair.

"Perhaps we can leave my men here to look through the rector's papers, Mrs Ellis, and you and I can have a chat in another room?

"Just scan through whatever papers you can find, sergeant. I'm not expecting to find many clues here, but you never know. Also, it would be nice to find that will – or at least a copy."

Mrs Ellis escorted Bryce to the next room, which he deduced was the dining room. This room also appeared to be very clean, the plain but serviceable furniture waxed and polished. Bryce wondered how many other rooms in the big house were so well maintained.

The DCI indicated that the housekeeper should sit down at the table, and he sat opposite.

"This must have come as a shock to you, Mrs Ellis," he began.

"That it did, sir," she replied. "In very good health, he was, as far as I knew. I went to the funeral yesterday, but I didn't fancy the wake, so after the burial I came back here. Then Mr Feeke rang from the Manor, on Squire's instructions, he said, to tell me Mr Watson had been taken to hospital. Well, I didn't rightly know what to do, but I knew Mr Watson had a brother – Mr Patrick – though he never visits here, so I found the number and told him. I'd hardly put the telephone down when the hospital rang and said the rector had died. I called Mr Patrick again, and passed on the news. He said to leave everything with him.

"Then Colonel Hardwicke himself rang this morning, and explained that the rector had been poisoned. Doesn't seem possible, sir."

Bryce observed that the housekeeper wasn't displaying the slightest signs of sorrow, her manner unaffected by any emotion. She evidently realised that he had noticed this, and explained:

"Although I was shocked, sir, I can't say that I'll grieve. Mr Watson was a difficult man to work for. He was very good at his job, I think; never shirked his duty in the parish. And he could be genuinely nice – but too often he could be really horrible. Jekyll and Hyde, I think they call it.

"It may strike you as selfish, sir, but my only real sorrow is for myself. I was employed by the rector, and I wasn't in my first flush of youth when he took me on. I'll probably be dismissed by his replacement."

Mrs Ellis whisked a hand at some imaginary fleck of dust on the table. "When Colonel Hardwicke rang this morning, he kindly told me that if the rector hadn't made any arrangements, he would cover my wages himself for three months. As he said, that would give time to see what a new rector might want, or to find another post. I don't hold out much hope of a new job at my age, and it's not pleasant to lose your job and your home at the same time."

"Yes, I see," said Bryce, feeling more than a little sorry for the downcast woman, burdened with worry for her future. "I hope whoever is next appointed comes here before making any decisions, sees how well-kept everything is, and says you can stay.

"Now, Mrs Ellis, as you were told, the rector was poisoned. It was probably strychnine, and if it was, then it was almost certainly in something he ate or drank during the wake."

"I'm glad to hear that, sir – I worried there might have been something amiss with the lunch I gave him yesterday."

"What was that, just as a matter of interest?"

"A plain omelette, with baked potatoes and chard. Tapioca to follow – because I already had the oven on for the potatoes," she replied. "But I'd made enough for Alice and me as well, so as it happened we all ate exactly the same yesterday."

"Well," said Bryce, "I don't know if you've heard about strychnine, but it has a very bitter taste, and poisoners have to hide the taste in something strongly flavoured. I think anyone eating your lunch would have noticed any poison immediately and stopped well before they could be harmed."

"I see," said Mrs Ellis. "Matter of fact, though, the rector didn't have what you might call a sensitive palate. For instance, he could never tell whether his new potatoes had been cooked with mint or not. Several times over the years he's asked me what meat he's eating. 'Is this beef or lamb, Mrs Ellis?' or 'is this pork or chicken?' he'd ask. Same with wine. He told me once that as he can't tell one red from another, he just buys the cheapest bottles. Apparently the colonel had called him a 'philistine' on one occasion."

Bryce considered what he had just been told. He wasn't sure whether this apparent defect would be sufficient to hide the presence of strychnine from the rector. If it was, then concentrating attention on the drinks might prove to be a serious error. He made a note to raise the point with one of his medical acquaintances.

"Now, Mrs Ellis, we come to a more difficult topic. You mentioned that the rector could be 'difficult', and in fact we've heard that he had upset or annoyed a number of people.

"Whether you got on with the man or not,

I'm sure you agree that it's not right for someone to murder him. Especially as people who kill once, often go on to do so again. But to catch the culprit, we need to find a motive. Someone who felt they had reason enough to do this dreadful crime.

"I need you to tell me about any incident that might have made someone dislike him. Any little thing, even if it wouldn't seem to be a reason for murder. This is in strict confidence, of course – nobody will ever know what you tell me."

Mrs Ellis didn't have the same compunction as the colonel when it came to speaking ill of the dead.

"I don't rightly know where to start. As I say, he was very good in many ways. But he was an awful hypocrite as well," said the housekeeper.

"You can ask Alice about this; she hadn't been here long when he made advances to her. She wanted to leave, but without a reference it would have been hard to get another post. I told the rector that if he tried it again we'd both leave together, and we'd tell everyone why.

"And a few months ago he started getting visits from that Vicky Anderson, from the New Farm. Far too many visits to be parish business, and he made a point of saying he didn't want to be disturbed while she was here. She's a married woman – and young enough to be his daughter.

"Then, even more hypocrisy over Mr Eccles. The rector might not have appreciated a fine wine, but he used to drink a good amount of whatever he did have. Yet only a week or so ago, he told me that Mr Eccles' shouldn't have a public house in the village, and that he was going get someone to stop him trading.

"I don't know much about money, sir – never had any to speak of. And I don't know how much the rector made, although I hear this is a very valuable living for its size. But I do know that he sometimes lent money. Not very much at any one time, I think. A few pounds here and there. But I hear that he charged a lot of interest.

"Again, you can ask Alice about this; she told me in confidence that her father was one who borrowed. He borrowed only three pounds, and had to pay back three pounds six shillings just four weeks later. I wasn't bad at arithmetic in school, and I reckon that's a yearly rate of over a hundred percent. He may not have been a moneylender in the temple, but it was near enough to my mind. I hope he's being held to account for it right now!"

The housekeeper suddenly looked as if she felt she had said too much and stopped, clamping her lips together.

"Thank you again, Mrs Ellis. What you have said corresponds with other things we have heard. Of course, it's quite possible that his murder may not be linked with any of them; it's very early days yet. Is there anything else you think I should know?"

The woman shook her head.

"Thank you then. Would you please ask

Alice to come and talk to me? But don't say what we've been talking about – I'd rather she started off without any warning."

The housekeeper departed. A few minutes later there was a tap on the door, and a girl let herself into the room. She was not in uniform, but was neatly dressed. Of a rather non-descript countenance, with hair of a colour which is sometimes described as 'mouse', she nevertheless had an appealingly wide-eyed and open manner. Bryce stood politely, as was his custom, and offered his hand.

"Come and sit down, Alice," he said. First, please tell me your full name, and a bit about yourself."

"My name is Alice Marwick, sir," she replied. "I'm twenty-three, and I've been here about two years. Before that, from when I left school, I was in service with Mrs Baxter at Poplar House – that's in the next village. But she died. Nobody has bought the house yet, and it's such a nice little place," she added, as though she felt obliged to make conversation.

Bryce, recognising her nervousness, proceeded gently. "Thank you, Alice. As you know, I'm trying to find out who poisoned the Rector. Part of doing that is finding out who had a motive – a reason – for killing him. Now, we have heard some things about him which weren't all good. Suppose you tell me about anything you know yourself, or know that other people have experienced. Things that might have given people a reason to dislike him."

Alice didn't look very happy, but nodded.

"Yes, sir, I understand what you want. I don't rightly like to say, though."

"Perhaps I can help you a little. I don't want to put words in your mouth, but would it be right that he perhaps tried to be a little too friendly towards you – in a completely unwelcome way?"

"Thank you, sir, yes, that's put it exactly. He tried to kiss me and... and more things...grabbing at me. I don't like to talk of it. Mrs Ellis warned him off good and proper though, and since then it's been all right. Like nothing ever happened, as far as he was concerned."

"We don't need to talk about that anymore, then. What about things that you might have heard about happening to someone else?"

With considerable reluctance, Alice brought out the visits from Mrs Anderson, and the exorbitant (although she didn't call it that) interest on the loan to her father.

"Those are the sort of things we've been told about by several other people. By the way, did your father know that the rector had pestered you?"

"Yes, he did. I told my Mum, and though I didn't want her to, she told Dad. He was hopping mad, and talked of 'sorting that man out'. He already had no respect for him 'cos of the borrowing. Anyhow, we talked it over, and in the end he could see that I really had to stay, and he spoke to Mrs Ellis and she told him what she'd done so it would never happen again."

Alice suddenly realised that she had been almost casting her father as a potential murderer.

"Oh but no, sir!" she cried. "Don't you go thinking Dad killed him. Rector messing with me was a year ago, and Dad had already paid the loan back by then. He wouldn't plot revenge all this time. And if he had it would only have been to give him a talking-to – never murder."

"I'm glad your father didn't take matters into his own hands, Alice," Bryce told her. "All I'm doing is building up a picture of the sort of man the rector was. Then we get a picture of who might have hated him. And I can tell you that we've already heard of several people who have a more recent – and maybe stronger – motive than your Dad.

"Now that the rector has gone, do you know what you'll do?"

"Not really, sir," said the girl, tears coming into her eyes for the first time. "I don't know of anywhere else hereabouts that I could go to, and I'm not drawn to the towns like some are. Squire rang this morning, and he said he'd pay our wages for three months unless something else came along. He said perhaps a new rector might want to take us on here."

Bryce thanked Alice for her help and wished her good luck for her future. After the maid had gone, Bryce sat in quiet contemplation for a while before going in search of his colleagues. They had just finished their search.

"Not much to report, sir," said Haig. "We found the will. It's in a sealed envelope, so we haven't read it. The only other thing is this ledger – a very business-like book, the sort that small firms use for their annual accounts. It seems the rector was in the habit of lending sums of money to his parishioners at usurious rates of interest. Another list of people with possible motives, sir?"

"Yes, I've just been hearing about the money lending. We'll talk about this later. Bring the ledger and the will, and we'll get off to the pub for the night."

Seeing a bellpush, he rang for the housekeeper. Alice came in answer to the call.

"We're going to leave now, Alice. All we're taking is this envelope, which is the rector's will; and this book, which seems to show about the money he lent to various people. Please tell Mrs Ellis. If the rector's brother comes you can tell him the same thing.

"The inquest will start in a day or two – do you know what an inquest is?"

"I think so sir. Isn't it where they decide how someone died?"

"Yes, that's roughly right. Well, at some time in a week or so it's just possible that you and Mrs Ellis may be called as witnesses. I think that's very unlikely, but it's nothing to worry about anyway."

CHAPTER 13

The three officers returned to the car. Kittow drove the quarter mile to the village, and parked outside the Dog and Partridge. Carrying their bags, the detectives made their way inside.

'Reception' was simply an open hatch giving access onto one end of the saloon bar. As Bryce appeared at the hatch, a man moved down the bar towards him.

"Ah, now, will you be our London police guests?"

Bryce confirmed this.

"Welcome one and all to the Dog, gentlemen. I'm Marcus Eccles, landlord here. If you would sign the register, I'll show you to your rooms.

Formalities completed, Eccles collected three keys from a row of hooks, and led the Yard men upstairs. Opening the first of three doors he said:

"All the rooms are identical, gentlemen, and

all face the back, looking over the countryside, so they're very quiet. Bathroom is at the end there. Now, you'll be wanting to eat, perhaps?"

All three officers nodded.

"Just come down to the bar when you're ready, then. We don't offer any choice – just the one hot dinner each day, but the wife will always do a ploughman's instead, if that's preferred. I believe you'll find our hot food is good, though."

He handed over the keys, and returned to the stairs.

Bryce looked through the door which the landlord had just unlocked. He saw an inviting interior, the sloping ceiling and exposed beams creating immediate character in the room. A well-filled eiderdown was folded back over a thick woollen blanket, with pristine cotton sheets and pillowcases showing at the head of the bedstead. A wardrobe and small dressing table completed the furniture, with a fluffy rag rug at the foot of the bed giving a burst of home-spun colour to the pleasant room.

The DCI turned and grinned at his companions. "I don't often do it, but today I'm going to pull rank and bag the bedroom nearest the bathroom. You're in here, Adam, with Alex as 'piggy in the middle'. Let's all clean up and meet in the saloon bar in twenty minutes."

Haig was first downstairs. The room was distinctly rustic, it's ceiling very low and very yellow, discoloured by countless pipes and cigarettes over the years. A narrow shelf just below the ceiling ran around the room, holding the biggest collection of Toby jugs that Haig had ever seen. He settled himself on a bar stool, one boot resting on the brass foot rail running the length of the bar, mentally betting himself that the public bar would have a spittoon. He resolved to glance in later to check.

The landlord, who was chatting to an elderly patron a little further along the bar, moved along to serve him.

"Pint of best bitter for me, please," said Haig. "And another for my boss. I'm not sure what our other colleague drinks, so better wait for him."

Eccles drew the two pints, and pointed to a blackboard. The evening's offering was chicken stew and dumplings, with mashed potatoes and calabrese, followed by apple and blackberry pie.

"I saw your names in the book, of course, but can you tell me which of you is which – and your ranks?" asked Eccles as he pulled the pints.

"The boss is Detective Chief Inspector Bryce, the young man is Detective Constable Kittow, and I'm Detective Sergeant Haig."

Before any further conversation ensued, Kittow appeared at the bar.

"What do you drink, Adam?" asked Haig.

"Bitter, please Sarge." Haig pushed the second pint towards Kittow, and nodded to the landlord, who drew a third pint ready for the DCI.

"That makes further orders simple," said

Haig, "we all drink the same."

He pointed the blackboard out to Kittow as Bryce joined them, wearing a faint, contented smile. Haig surmised that his boss had been on the telephone to his wife. He himself had gone downstairs to call Fiona before even looking in his room.

The DCI picked up the pint that Eccles pushed towards him. "Your good health, landlord," he said.

"Thank you, sir, but I don't doubt you've got me down as a suspect in this murder," replied Eccles. "That being so, if you want to talk to me, we can do it anytime that suits you."

Bryce smiled. "Well, I can't deny that you are on the list of suspects, Mr Eccles, but as you can imagine, that list is quite a long one. However, it would be helpful to get your interview out of the way."

"We'll serve you dinner in the private dining room, and when you've finished I can talk to you in there," said the landlord obligingly. "Like the rest of the pub, it's got thick walls and thick doors – the soundproofing is very good."

"Excellent, thanks for the offer; we'll do that. Shouldn't take very long. Now, however, we're looking forward to sampling your food whenever you're ready."

Eccles went to the kitchen to give the order.

"I hope you know something about railways – especially steam locomotives – and cricket,

Adam," said Haig over the top of his pint. "You should know that the guvnor and I are both keen on them."

Bryce laughed. "Quite true," he said. "I have to admit that, having selected Alex to work with me mainly on the basis that he is a non-smoker, I was pleasantly surprised to learn that he shared those interests."

"If you checked on my smoking habits, guv, you'll know that I don't smoke either," said Kittow.

"I certainly did check," smiled Bryce.

"Oh!" Kittow was surprised that the DCI had bothered to investigate his habits. "I don't smoke because I don't enjoy it, and also because it costs money," he said. "That's always been two very good reasons for me not to bother with it. Now I see there may be another advantage!

"As for the railways, I'm pretty sure that I'll not come up to your standards, guv. But if it might get me into your good books, I can say that as a kid a year or two before the war, I used to buy a platform ticket at St John's station in Lewisham where we lived – very busy lines through it, although probably most trains didn't bother to stop there – and go and watch the trains pass by. Especially the steam ones, of which there were a lot at that time. I wanted to be an engine driver, of course, like most of my friends.

"We used to see the old Maunsell locomotives like the Schools and the Lord Nelsons. Nowadays, it must be even more interesting with

Bulleid's beautiful 'spam cans', and his funny-looking Q1s steaming past.

"As for cricket, as a Kentish Man I obviously support Kent, and when they're playing at Beckenham I get over there when I can."

"Ah, a Kentish Man. That means you were born to the west of the county, doesn't it?" asked Bryce.

"That's right, guv, west of the Medway. Those born to the east are Men of Kent. Not many outsiders know about that distinction. Some people argue over whether the river is the true dividing line; others argue about the origins of the terms; and for many years there's been a few snobs who maintain that Men of Kent are superior in all respects." Kittow swallowed some bitter. "Complete tosh, obviously.

"But going back to the railways; if we aren't talking about the Southern Railway, as it used to be, then you're bound to find me a bit ignorant!"

"Not at all; we'll just put you down as having specialist knowledge about the Southern," laughed Haig, happy, like Bryce, that Kittow would 'fit in' with the team when off-duty.

"Do you have many people staying?" asked Bryce, as the landlord strayed close to them again.

"Comes in bursts, really," replied Eccles. "Maybe we're empty for a week or ten days, then suddenly all four rooms are taken for the next week. Usually, it's little groups of visitors, like you gentlemen, rather than individual bookings.

The university sometimes recommends the Dog to people coming to the city for seminars and such. The Randolph often gets full, and some folk prefer to get out of the city anyway. And then we sometimes get a few people coming for a cycling or driving tour of the Cotswolds, that sort of thing."

He moved away again.

"Well, guv," said Haig, "this is the third place I've stayed with you now. Nothing'll ever beat the White Hart, unless one day we get billeted at Gleneagles or somewhere like that. But, subject to tasting the food, this looks a lot better than the wretched Fitzroy Arms."

"Agreed," said Bryce. "However, we have to take what the local force offers. Or, as in this case probably, what happens to be available within a five-mile radius."

He signalled to the landlord for three more pints.

Haig mentioned the lych gate he and the DCI had seen earlier, saying how he had never seen a dual-purpose one before.

Kittow was immediately interested. "I lost two uncles on the Somme," he said. "Never knew them, of course – they died ten years before I was born. Their names are on the memorial near their home, and on that huge memorial in Thiepval, but no one knows where their resting places are." He took a long pull at his pint and said, "Before we leave Mistram, I'd like to look at this lychgate, guv, if we have time."

"I'll make sure you get time to do that, Adam," promised Bryce. "I was on a cycling holiday in Picardy in 1935, and I went to see the Thiepval memorial. It was only a few years old then, and the facing of white Portland stone was gleaming. As I'm sure you know, it only records the names of those, like your uncles, with no known grave.

"I'm a great fan of Lutyens' work, and Thiepval has to be a triumph at least as great as his buildings in New Delhi. If you're ever in Manchester, go and look at the Midland Bank building. Or if you want to see one of the most beautiful Arts and Crafts houses in the country, go to Goddards in Surrey. Some say he was the greatest English architect since Wren; others – like me – say he was the greatest ever."

He gave a self-deprecating wave of the hand. "Apologies, gentlemen, I get carried away sometimes."

"Oh no sir," exclaimed Kittow. "I find that sort of thing interesting. Wasn't he the man who did the Cenotaph in Whitehall?"

"That's right. Actually, I think there are over forty other Lutyens war memorials dotted around the country. It's said that he designed the Cenotaph in six hours – compared to the twenty years or so he spent on New Delhi."

Eccles returned, and announced that their first course was ready. He led them through to a compact dining room containing only a single table with chairs for six, and a sideboard.

Piping hot plates were already waiting for the food, and as the detectives took their seats a large woman carrying a tray emerged from what was evidently the kitchen.

"Good evening, gentlemen," she said, beaming with friendliness. "I'm Edith Eccles."

With practised efficiency she removed and set down three round earthenware crocks, each with its own serving spoon or ladle.

"Now, there's a bell on the wall to press when you've finished. I see you've brought your ale through – do you wish for anything further to drink before I leave?"

All three men declined. The landlady hovered a moment and then said:

"Eccles tells me you're going to interview him later. I'd just like to say that I was in the room when the rector was taken ill, so if you want to talk to me…"

"Thank you, Mrs Eccles, that's a very good suggestion. We'll talk to you straight after we see your husband, if that's convenient."

When the door had closed behind her Bryce, regardless of the landlord's claim about soundproofing, spoke quietly:

"She may not have been anywhere near the rector yesterday, and I don't imagine she saw anything suspicious. But I bet she doesn't miss much around the village, and perhaps we'll get a bit more gossip from her. We have to find a credible motive somehow."

All three men now turned towards the food.

"Let's serve ourselves from the nearest crock, and then rotate them," said Bryce.

In no time at all, each man was attacking a generously filled plate. Silence fell as their attention was given over to satisfying their hunger.

"This is all uncommonly good, guv," said Haig at last.

Kittow licked his lips and agreed enthusiastically, "I'm surprised Mrs Eccles doesn't fit a little anchor to her dumplings they're so light – I swear I'm having to fight to keep this one on my plate!"

Bryce laughingly nodded. It was a fact that the food – although simply prepared and served – was first rate. The chicken stew had carrot and shallots swimming in the savoury golden gravy; the mashed potato was a steaming hot, fluffy cloud; and the calabrese was perfectly cooked and even a little buttered. The three men all agreed they were more than happy with their Hobson's choice.

When their initial appetite was dulled, they re-started their conversation from the bar, discussing a variety of topics before ringing the bell.

Mrs Eccles promptly returned to clear away the plates and crocks, and was pleased to take their compliments. Disappearing with the dirty dishes, she soon returned with another tray bearing another crock – this one a large oval – holding the apple and blackberry pie.

"All the fruit is from our own trees and brambles, and the eggs from our own hens for the custard," she said, lifting a jug off the tray and passing out bowls and spoons. "I don't think this will disappoint you either, gentlemen."

The conversation remained general for the rest of the meal, but as soon as each man had pushed back his bowl, the DCI told his colleagues the detail of his chats with Mrs Ellis and Alice Marwick at the rectory.

"Also, I've looked at the will. Not a long document, and it doesn't give us any idea of the size of Watson's estate. Colonel Hardwicke said that there was some unusual arrangement attached to this living, which provided a decent amount of money. And he doesn't seem to have been a big spender. Apart from a legacy of £50 to Mrs Ellis, the residue goes to the Parochial Church Council for the upkeep of St Anselm's. His brother isn't mentioned. I don't think the hope of an inheritance on anyone's part is a motive in this case.

"I've also glanced through the loan book. There are twenty-three names, several appearing more than once. Alice's father's name is there, as she said it would be. The first entry is about three years ago, although I suppose there could have been an earlier book. No amount lent has been greater than five pounds. Most loans have been repaid – in fact there are only two outstanding. Two happy people, I imagine, as I don't suppose anyone will chase them for repayment. I'll check with the guest list tomorrow to see if either of the borrowers even went to the wake yesterday.

"Most significantly for us, none of the people in the parlour yesterday appear in the book, so I don't think it takes us any further except in helping us to know the type of man the rector was. Lending money to help people out is one thing – charging crippling rates of interest is something else.

"Actually, given what happened to Alice, and her father's reaction, I also need to check the guest list to see if he was present somewhere. But even if he was still feeling like murder a year after the incident, and even if he was there yesterday, I can't see how he could have done it."

"Like I said at the house, guv – I could dig myself in here very nicely. How long do you reckon we'll have to stay?" enquired Kittow.

"Lap of the gods, Adam. We haven't got very far as yet. But, as the saying goes, tomorrow is another day.

"Assuming you both want coffee, do you want something with it?"

Both men declined, and Bryce rose and pressed the bell again.

When Mrs Eccles returned Bryce ordered the coffees and asked her to inform her husband that they were ready for him.

Eccles arrived a few minutes later, bringing the coffee with him. He placed the tray in front of Kittow, on the unspoken assumption that the most junior would pour.

"Thank you, Mr Eccles, do sit down," said Bryce, pointing to a chair where all three policemen could observe him. Kittow swiftly sorted out the coffees.

"This won't take very long," Bryce continued. "Just as for the other people we've seen, there are two parts to the interview.

"First, thinking back to yesterday afternoon. Please describe what happened after you first entered the breakfast room – that's the room where the food was laid out."

"Well, Edith and me, we were told to go into one of two rooms, and we chose that one – could just as well have been the one next door, it was a toss of a coin in the head, really. We were met by young Mrs Hardwicke, the colonel's daughter-in-law. I'd spoken to her several times over the last few years, although I didn't properly know her, of course. Anyway, she welcomed us very nicely and told us to take a plate and help ourselves, and she pointed out where there was drink laid out, too.

"By the time we'd sorted our food and drink, the breakfast room was starting to fill up and we thought we'd better make space for others. So we went through the doors into the next room. Just ahead of us, Giles Anderson had gone through with Mr Dauntsey. They're both patrons of the

Dog, and I know them well, so we went to talk to them at the far end of the room. Then Adelaide Wilkin – she's the postmistress – followed us in, and she and Edith decided to sit down by the window. They're old friends.

"Anyhow, we men had hardly started to talk when Tony Bixby came through with his fiancée. Tony drinks in the Dog; Doreen doesn't. But I know her by sight, like I do all the locals.

"Then it started to fill up even more. An old boy came along with another man who introduced himself as the colonel's lawyer. I'd never met them before. The old boy doesn't live near here. He said he'd known the colonel for over fifty years.

"Is this the sort of thing you want to know, chief inspector?"

"Very much so. Do go on, please."

"Well, the seven of us were just talking, like about what a nice lady Mrs Beth had been. Then the rector comes and joins the group."

Eccles fell silent. The policemen waited. Eventually, the landlord continued.

"Rector had hardly got there when another dog-collared man arrived, a lot younger. Edwards his name was. None of us – and I think that includes the rector – had seen him before, but he said he was Mrs Beth's cousin or something."

Once again, Eccles fell silent. This time, Bryce helped him out.

"I have some idea of why you are hesitant, Mr Eccles. I suggest we move on to the second part of the interview, and we can come back later to what happened in the parlour.

"We've heard, from several different sources, that a number of local people may have had reasons not to respect the rector, shall we say. And perhaps different people had different reasons. What can you tell us that might confirm what others have told us, or that might even add to our knowledge?"

Eccles bared his teeth in a sneering smile.

"Oh, you're quite right about the man having enemies. There was me, for a start. I'm not saying, of course, that any of us would have killed him, but I can't deny there were a few who despised him."

Once Eccles heard that others had criticised the rector, he seemed much happier to expound on his own disagreement with the man. He described in detail what the rector had said about trying to have his licence revoked and get him evicted, the cause for which was allegedly that there had been an incident a couple of months before, involving three or four drunken patrons leaving the public house. It seemed the rector had happened to observe this.

"You've confirmed what we've heard before, Mr Eccles, and that's very helpful. Now, we are trying to build up a picture of the rector. What else can you tell us about him that might help us? Either what you know for a fact – like your own disagreement – or what you've heard across the bar or elsewhere."

Bryce waited with an expectant look on his face. Eccles hesitated. Then, having clearly made up his mind, he started to talk again:

"It's a very strange thing, sir. In many ways the rector did a lot of good in the parish, and there's probably a fair few who'd swear he's a saint. But there's no denying he had this black side to him.

"I don't know what you've heard already, and I'd as soon not be the one who tells you anything new. But there are those who had cause to loathe him.

"Take Isaac Marwick. His daughter went to work for the rector when old Mrs Baxter died in the next village. Well, Alice hadn't been there a month when the rector assaulted her. Isaac found out, and he was madder than a nest of hornets what's been poked with a stick."

Having apparently put his reticence to one side, the landlord crossed his arms, sat back in his chair, and went on disapprovingly:

"Then it seems that the rector had an affair with Victoria Anderson, Silas's wife. How long it was going on I have no idea, but everyone seems to know about it now. Not sure if Silas threw her out, but she's not living at the farm now. So I reckon you can add 'home wrecker' to the rector's charge sheet."

Eccles also knew about the upset about Doreen not being allowed a church wedding –

apparently Bixby had been ranting about it in the pub a few nights before.

The landlord went on to say that the rector lent money to various people, and allegedly got very nasty if they didn't pay their instalments. However, although he gave the names of a few of the borrowers, he was unable to identify any who had actually been threatened.

"Thank you, Mr Eccles. It all helps. Now that we've got your own disagreement out of the way, let's go back to what happened yesterday. You told us that the rector joined your little group, and that another clergyman came along shortly after. What happened then?"

The landlord bridled and shook his head. "For myself, I couldn't believe that the man would have the brass neck to come over and join a group that had Silas, Tony, Doreen, and me in it."

Bryce noted that Eccles didn't include Dauntsey's name, so it seemed that knowledge of that particular spat had not been widely disseminated. But the fact was that Dauntsey's presence simply added to the DCI's own feeling of disbelief at the rector's choosing to join the group at all.

"Anyway," the landlord continued, "from the moment he arrived, I can tell you that he never addressed a single word to me, or to Silas, or to Tony. Only time he spoke to Doreen was to tell her to fetch him some wine. The rest of the time he pointedly spoke to the solicitor, the other priest, and the old boy. They were all polite though, and not above talking to us when they could. Come to think of it, I don't remember him saying anything to Mr Dauntsey, either.

"I can't speak for the others, but I felt like going out to another room. Trouble was, we were all a bit jammed in – and also Edith was sitting happy with her friend.

"Anyway, I stayed put. Then, the colonel himself came in and made his way over to us. He didn't say much, just greeted us all as a group, really. He said something to Tony and Doreen about their engagement, and told us all about the will, and then he moved away again.

"A bit later, the rector sort of doubled up, and started groaning, and fell to the floor. Doreen screamed and the two old soldiers moved us out of the room. Someone fetched Dr Ford, and the rector was taken away to hospital. Last thing we heard was that it was his appendix. Nobody thought it was anything fatal."

He paused, and the three policemen mentally reviewed what he had said. Everything seemed to fit with what other witnesses had said. Haig interposed a question:

"We understand that the rector asked for a cup of coffee, and that one of the grandchildren brought it for him. Was that before or after the colonel was with you?"

Eccles thought for a second.

"Definitely after," he replied. "Perhaps ten

minutes after. And then I suppose it was another ten minutes before he collapsed."

"One last question, Mr Eccles. Did you see anyone doing anything which, with hindsight, was strange? Reaching across the table towards the rector's food or drink, for example?"

"Can't say I did, no. I've thought about this a lot since we heard the man was dead, of course, and tried to relive the scene in my mind. But no. I reckon it wouldn't have been too hard for someone to do it, though, is the most I can say.

"And before you ask, chief inspector, yes, I'm not sorry the man is dead. But I didn't kill him, and I honestly have no idea who did."

Bryce thanked the landlord again, and asked him to see if his wife could spare a few minutes.

Mrs Eccles returned. The interview was largely a waste of everyone's time, as she could only repeat most of the rumours concerning the rector, and had seen no interference with his food or drink.

When she had retired again, Bryce outlined the programme for the morning.

"Sergeant Jarvis is coming to collect me at eight thirty. I'll get him to take me to the manor first, so I can check the guest lists again, and then telephone to try to make appointments with McKay and Dauntsey. Jarvis can drive me around to see them. Hicks too, time permitting. I need to see Bixby as well, but no doubt he'll be around the garden somewhere.

"While I'm on the telephone, I'll try to contact the Reverend Edwards, and tell him you are coming.

"I want you two to take the bits and pieces to Hendon. I suggest you leave about eight thirty too. When you been to the lab, go and see if you can find Edwards. I'll copy out the address and telephone number the colonel gave me – it seems to be his landlady's address – and also the name of his church.

"Now, I'm for an early night."

CHAPTER 14

The following morning, Bryce and his colleagues were enjoying an excellent breakfast when Mrs Eccles came to the table:

"Telephone for you, chief inspector," she said.

The call lasted only two minutes, and on returning to his seat Bryce passed on to his colleagues what he had learned.

"That was the local superintendent. They worked on the analysis of the autopsy samples overnight, and he was reporting on the result. As expected, Watson died from a massive dose of strychnine. The estimate the doc gave to you was pretty accurate, Adam – nearer two grains than one, and less than one grain can be fatal.

"One thing that arose from my talk with Mrs Ellis which I don't think I passed on to you last night, is that the rector had a rather underdeveloped palate. Apparently he couldn't distinguish one sort of meat from another, for example. I'm going to telephone the Lab people to see if they have any experience of such a thing, and whether they think that means he might not notice the sort of dose of strychnine which a normal person would. I'm hoping that they might have an answer by the time you get to Hendon later in the morning. But it may be such a rare condition that there is no precedent. In a way, I hope this makes no difference, because obviously if he couldn't taste the stuff then my assumption about it being in the wine or coffee goes out of the window!"

A few minutes before eight thirty, the three officers were leaving the Dog and Partridge as Sergeant Jarvis drove up in a new-looking Wolseley 6/80 police car, complete with a bell on the front. Jarvis was evidently most pleased with the car, and it soon transpired that as he never usually drove police vehicles, he was more than happy to do so today.

After Haig and Kittow had left for London, Jarvis explained that Superintendent Denton had said that he wouldn't be much use to the DCI with only a bicycle, and so had personally allocated this almost-new car for the use of the Yard team.

"Very thoughtful of Mr Denton," remarked Bryce. "We're off to the manor first, please, Jarvis."

Feeke let them into the house.

"We've only come to make a few telephone calls," said Bryce, "and then we're off to see various people. But as a courtesy perhaps you'd just let the colonel know we'll be in the study for a little while."

Feeke bowed, once again appreciating that the DCI understood how to 'do things in the way they should be done'.

The two officers turned into the study, and Feeke continued with his message to the drawing room.

Bryce told the sergeant to take a seat, while he himself looked through the two lists of guests and compared them with the names in Watson's loan ledger. First, he satisfied himself that Mr Marwick had not been present at the wake – or at least, neither list contained his name.

Next, he went through every other name in the book, but found that in fact none of the borrowers had been present. This seemed surprising, given the size of the wake and the smallness of the parish, but he thought that perhaps they simply chose to avoid the rector – who would inevitably have been present. Or perhaps some of those involved might have even moved to get away from his clutches. He put the matter to the back of his mind, and picked up the telephone.

Fifteen minutes later, he had successfully made four appointments to see the agent, the solicitor, Major Hicks, and Silas Anderson, in that order.

He had also managed to speak to Mr Edwards' landlady, who said that her lodger was out, and she would pass on the message that two officers were coming to see him when he arrived for his lunch about noon.

Finally, he had spoken to one of the medics at the Hendon lab, about the matter of the non-sensitive palate. The doctor said he'd never come across such a case, but his interest was sufficiently piqued for him to promise to talk to someone in Harley Street.

Satisfied with the way his telephone calls and appointments had all fallen neatly into place, Bryce was ready to give the sergeant his instructions.

"Right, Jarvis, I need to you take me to the estate office first. I gather it's at the Home Farm – how far is that?"

Jarvis estimated it was probably only half a mile as the crow flies, but more like two miles by road. As they passed through the hall on their way back to the car, Colonel Hardwicke appeared. Greeting the two men, he asked the inevitable question about progress.

Bryce was not in the habit of sharing information with 'outsiders', much less someone who technically remained a suspect. However, he had sympathy for the man who had not only just lost his wife, but had a murder committed in his house on the day he buried her. He responded with as much as he felt was wise.

"Not much progress yet colonel. We've seen four or five witnesses, and we're off now to see some more. My men have gone to London with the potential evidence for the laboratory to analyse.

"The only bit of news won't come as a surprise: Mr Watson ingested nearly two grains of strychnine, probably an unsurvivable quantity, even if your GP had instantly used a stomach pump."

The colonel grunted. "Poor old Ford, he muttered, "he'll not live this down. High time he retired, anyway.

"Thank you, Bryce. Good luck with your investigations today. I hope you were looked after at the Dog?"

Assuring him that they had indeed been well looked after, Bryce and Jarvis escaped to the car.

Jarvis drove competently enough for a man who, as he said, rarely had a chance to drive a police car.

He wasn't particularly shy in front of his superior from London, and during the short journey regaled the DCI with stories about local 'villains'. Bryce wondered how the sergeant would find life in the Met – where felons tended to commit rather more serious offences than poaching, fishing without a licence, being drunk and disorderly, or shooting game out of season or on a Sunday.

Arriving at the Home Farm, Jarvis indicated that the estate office door was just around a corner of the building in front of them.

"You can come in with me, sergeant," said Bryce. "But I don't expect you to ask questions; just take notes of anything that seems relevant."

James Dauntsey met the two men at the office door. He knew Jarvis of course, and Bryce introduced himself as they shook hands. Dauntsey ushered them to chairs, and offered coffee, which both officers accepted. He called out the order to someone in the adjoining room.

Bryce made a quick assessment of the agent, and saw a handsome man in his forties, bearded but going thin on top, wearing a tweed suit that had lost a lot of its shape and nap. He formed an impression of a man for whom appearance was not a pressing priority.

"Well, Mr Dauntsey," began Bryce, "you know why we're here, presumably. Mr Watson died of strychnine poisoning. You were one of about nine people within range of him, during the time he must have ingested the poison."

The agent looked calmly at the DCI.

"This isn't the time to joke," he said at last, "I certainly understand my position. But I suppose as long as I'm only one of a decent-sized group of suspects, my appearance at the Assizes isn't imminent!"

"Very true," replied Bryce. "But I do hope to whittle the number down fairly rapidly.

"Anyway, I've already seen a fair number of the group, and one way or another we'll interview the rest today. I'm going to take a different tack with you, and come straight out with something. We've learned, from various sources, that Watson had ways of upsetting people. You'll appreciate that we need to find someone with a motive. I know that you, for example, crossed swords with him about your professed atheism."

Dauntsey smiled faintly, and didn't seem at all put out.

"I don't know who told you, chief inspector. The colonel, I imagine, although I shouldn't be surprised to hear that the rector had spread the matter around. What happened was this. I'm not a churchgoer, and a week or so ago the rector tackled me about it – some guff about 'setting a good example'. I don't know what set him off – I've been here for several years, and he's never raised the matter before.

"Anyway, I know many people who attend out of duty, rather than true religious conviction, and to me that's a tad hypocritical. The rector must have been aware of that some of his flock were simply paying lip-service; but perhaps he only cared about posteriors on pews.

"As for those who don't attend, they possibly either can't spare the time, or simply can't be bothered. When the old sinner tackled me, I could have found all sorts of excuses – that I was of another faith, or allergic to candle fumes, or that my piles wouldn't permit me to sit through his services. But I chose to tell him the truth – I don't go because I am an atheist. Not just agnostic, a full-blown atheist. I don't go around proselytising, so the matter had nothing to do with him.

"Incidentally, I didn't enter the church for the funeral service yesterday. I waited outside, talking to one of the gardeners and patting the colonel's dogs, and then attended the interment out of respect to Beth."

At this point a middle-aged woman entered the room pushing a small trolley. Bryce and Jarvis rose.

"This is my wife, Pandora, chief inspector. Officially, she is my extremely efficient secretary, but actually she could do my job at least as well as I can. She was at the wake too, but had the good sense to go into the drawing room."

"Nice to meet you, Mr Bryce, and good morning sergeant," said Mrs Dauntsey, handing out cups of coffee and offering milk and sugar.

"I heard what my husband has said, and I absolutely agree. James, I hope you go on and tell the police about some of the rector's other peccadilloes, as we might euphemistically call them."

With that parting comment, she smiled and left the room and closed the door. There was a short pause as the three men stirred their drinks.

"I'll just finish about the rector and me," said Dauntsey. "He was absolutely livid when I mentioned atheism, spluttering and shouting, and threatening me with everything from the wrath of his God to the wrath of my employer. I had him down as the sort who would happily burn someone at the stake for worshipping the 'wrong' god, never mind one who had no god at all.

"Anyway, I had no fear of his first threat, and very little of his second. I've always found the colonel to be a reasonable and fair-minded man. That observation seems to have been well-founded; although I haven't had a chance to talk to him about this yet, it seems he sent the rector packing. Watson came round here the next day, ranting on about the squire not doing his duty.

"I was scrupulously polite, but that just seemed to inflame the man more."

"I'm sure the colonel will give you the detail himself, but I don't see why I shouldn't tell you this – he backed you to the hilt," said Bryce.

"Anyway, the obvious question to you is this. Did you feel so antagonistic towards the Rector that you decided to kill him?"

"Certainly not! I'll admit to actively disliking him, yes – and I consider I had good reason. But I didn't hate him enough to even wish him dead – let alone to kill him."

"It appears that he may have been poisoned through something being added to his wine or his coffee. Did you observe anything untoward?"

"No. When he fell, I thought immediately that his symptoms looked like those involving poison – strychnine particularly – that I had read about. Incidentally, Ford was useless, as usual. Anyway, I'd replayed the scene in my mind even before I heard the man was dead, but I just didn't see anything at all suspicious."

"Regarding your wife's remark, Mr Dauntsey. As I said earlier, we have already heard details of a number of – let's call them incidents – which don't show the late rector in a good light.

"I don't want us to waste each other's time. I'll tell you we've heard about money lending, adultery, attempts to bar the publican, refusal to marry people, and making unwanted advances. If you can add any other 'peccadilloes', as your wife put it, to the list, then I'd like to hear. Otherwise, I suggest we leave the subject."

Dauntsey smiled. "I'd certainly heard of cases involving the first four, and I'm not surprised to hear of the fifth. But I can't add anything to those."

"One last thing. Were you surprised when the rector joined your little cluster of people, knowing as you seem to, that you weren't the only person who had reason to dislike him?"

The land agent now spoke with considerable animation, "I certainly was! I half-expected him to start on one or more of us, and I was prepared for a public row. But he studiously ignored me – and Eccles, and Anderson, and Bixby and Doreen. He just pointedly addressed remarks to Major Hicks and Travis McKay, and the curate from London, none of whom I imagine had any inkling of the inter-personal upsets. I'd like to think they thought he was being incredibly rude, though. The curate chap actually said very little, but McKay and Hicks did their best to include the rest of us."

Asking Dauntsey to thank his wife for the coffee, Bryce stood to leave, and they shook hands again.

Back in the car, Bryce asked Jarvis if he knew where Mr McKay's office was.

"Oh, yes, sir, it's in the town square."

"Good, let's go there now. What did you make of Mr Dauntsey, sergeant? Incidentally, I suppose that business of the rector's habits was news to you?"

"Oh, I knew about some of the goings on, sir. But there was never, so far as I knew, anything actually criminal. It's not illegal to lend money, nor to commit adultery. And when there might have been an offence, like the business with Alice Marwick, nobody would lay a complaint. I didn't know about Mr Dauntsey's run-in, though – but again that wouldn't have been a police matter unless there'd have been a breach of the peace.

"But in answer to your question, sir, I don't get a feeling that Mr Dauntsey is a killer. Mind you," he laughed, "to be honest I've never yet met one, so you maybe shouldn't set too much store by my opinion!"

Bryce laughed with the sergeant, but agreed with his assessment. Over the next few miles, as they drove towards the town, the two engaged in friendly conversation.

In the town, Jarvis easily found a parking

place in the square.

"Different state of affairs on market day, sir," he remarked, "the whole of this is under stalls and barrows. You'd have to park a quarter of a mile away, at least."

He led the DCI to an office nearby. The frontage of this side of the marketplace was almost continuous over at least a hundred yards. Bryce thought that it dated back to the early nineteenth century, and was probably designed originally to be a mixture of commercial premises and domestic residences – as it still seemed to be. Most of the frontage was liberally smothered with climbers – ivy and wisteria. The whole block was attractive – and when the wisteria was in flower the effect must have been stunning.

The two front windows of this office were each etched with 'McKay & Opie, Solicitors and Commissioners for Oaths'. The property looked to be in excellent repair, with pristine stone and paintwork. The two officers went up the steps and through the front door.

Bryce tapped on an open hatch in the hallway, and was greeted by a young lady seated at a 'sit up and beg' typewriter. Seeing the uniformed sergeant behind Bryce, she immediately stood and said:

"You must be Chief Inspector Bryce. If you'd like to take a seat in the waiting room on the other side of the hall, gentlemen, I'll tell Mr McKay that you are here."

The waiting room could have been for a Harley Street consultant, or an upmarket dentist, mused Bryce, eyeing the neatly placed collection of Country Life and similar magazines. He guessed that this firm probably specialised in handling wealthy clients, and estates like Mistram. Few – if any – people charged with a criminal offence would ever pass through this room, he thought.

They had hardly had time to sit down when the door opened, and a short, bald-headed man entered. Pushing his gold-rimmed spectacles back up his nose with one hand, he offered his other hand in greeting.

"'Morning gentlemen," he said. "Travis McKay."

The trio shook hands and McKay escorted them back through the hall and up the stairs into a large and very pleasant room overlooking the square.

"Do sit down," McKay invited them.

"You have a fine outlook here, Mr McKay," said Bryce as he compared the view from his own office at Scotland Yard with the solicitor's. "You are the senior partner, presumably?"

"Correct, chief inspector. But I'm not the original McKay. My grandfather founded the firm back in the nineteenth century. His junior partner was Michael Opie, whose grandson is, like me, a partner now. Albert Hardwicke's grandfather initially appointed this firm to handle a few matters, and he gradually transferred all the estate and private matters to us. We carry out similar work for a number of other clients, and smaller scale civil work for anybody else.

"Well, it's a sorry state of affairs that's brought you both here," continued McKay. "Poor Hardwicke; burying Beth and effectively hosting a murder on the same day. Good thing he's so robust – and has his excellent children and in-laws around him. I imagine you want to ask me whether I put poison in Watson's food?"

"Nothing I like better than people coming to the point straight away," smiled Bryce. "What's your answer?"

"No, I didn't, is my answer. And, anticipating your next question, I didn't see anyone else doing it either. But I have to say that it wouldn't have needed any skilful legerdemain to carry out the operation. We were in a fairly tight group at that end of the parlour, and people kept reaching towards the table to pick up or set down a plate or glass."

"Yes, so we gather from others," said Bryce. "We also understand that the rector was prone to what one party has called 'peccadilloes'. Involvement with women – willing or otherwise; money lending; and what might be termed vendettas against certain individuals."

"I live ten miles away, chief inspector, and don't frequent the Dog and Partridge. I have business dealings with Dauntsey, and obviously with Albert, but I've never heard any gossip from either of them. I only met Watson perhaps once year, always at Albert's table. Can't say I warmed to the man, and as Albert always seemed to seat him as far from the head of the table as possible, perhaps Albert didn't either.

"So no, I've heard nothing of these peccadilloes. I can, however, tell you that Watson, despite several reminders, has never paid an account I sent him over two years ago. I trust you won't think that soured relationship with the deceased amounts to a motive!"

"Within these four walls," Bryce continued, "as far as motive is concerned, all the other matters we've learned about would rank higher than your dispute – but not one of them seems sufficient to drive a sane person to commit murder.

"I'll just ask this. Watson was in your group for well over half an hour, I understand. Obviously one or more conversations were going on. I appreciate you don't know him that well, but did anything strike you about his general demeanour, or his attitude towards any of the others present?"

The solicitor thought for a moment, his lips in a moue.

"I thought he was discourteous," he said at last. "Bloody rude, in fact. He seemed to ignore those of a lower class, even though they were standing with him as guests in the house. Before the wake, I'd never met any of those – the affable landlord from the pub, a nice pair of youngsters who work for Hardwicke, and a local farmer. He only really seemed to address Hicks and me – I've met Hicks several times over many years. Watson also spoke to the other clergyman with us, but hardly got any response. And the clergyman also came from a landed background, or so he told us initially. Actually, Dauntsey himself comes from a noted county family, and was also ignored, so perhaps it wasn't simply a class thing. Anyway, I tried to keep the others included, and so did Dauntsey and Hicks, although whether that was in response to Watson's rudeness or simply their innate courtesy, I can't say."

Bryce nodded, then rose.

"Thank you," he said. "I can't say you've provided a breakthrough, but it's always good to get pictures from later witnesses which don't contradict those from earlier ones. We'll need a formal statement from you at some stage, but there's no hurry. I'm not sure when the inquest will be opened, but it's almost certain that I'll have to ask for an adjournment anyway."

"Ah," said McKay. "Well, it so happens that my partner, Hugh Opie, is the part-time coroner for this area. It was from him that I heard about Watson's death, actually.

"He isn't in the office this morning, so I can't introduce you. But if you like I'll ask him if he can delay opening for a few days, to give you a bit more time?"

"Much appreciated," replied the DCI,

reflecting that, as ever, contacts were everything in smoothing paths.

McKay escorted the two officers to the front door, and there was a further round of hand shaking.

"Is there a decent little café or eatery here, sergeant?" Bryce asked Jarvis as they stood on the pavement. "I'm sure you could do with a bite, and I know I could."

Jarvis pointed at an establishment across the square. "There's that, sir – the Copper Kettle Tea Rooms. They do a light lunch – soups, cold meat pie, that sort of thing. And their afternoon teas are delicious. No licence, though."

"Sounds just the job. I don't approve of drinking at lunchtime anyway – dulls the brain."

CHAPTER 15

At about the time Bryce and Jarvis were sitting down to their soup and sandwich lunch at the Copper Kettle, Haig and Kittow were in Ilford. They had left the material for analysis at the Hendon lab, and been handed a scribbled note to take back to Bryce. It read *'Sorry – no data on the taste business as yet. Making further enquiries. P.'*

Kittow turned into a road lined with small semi-detached houses from the nineteen-twenties or thirties, and pulled up outside number seventeen. The two men walked the few feet up the path, and Haig knocked. A diminutive lady opened the door. Before Haig could speak, she intoned in an adenoidal voice:

"You must be the policemen come to see Reverend Edwards. He'll be back for his meal in about ten minutes. Follow me – you can wait in the garden."

With this, she stood back and held open the door for them to pass, pointing a bony but imperiously commanding finger first at the door mat, and then at sheets of freshly laid newspaper covering the lino in the passageway.

Haig and Kittow wiped their feet and followed her through the house, stepping only on the newspaper pathway until they reached the back door. Again, their nameless guide opened the door for them to pass, then shut it firmly behind them.

The word 'garden' was a complete misnomer for the few square yards of crazy paving at the back of the house. In the absence of any sort of bench or ornamental wall on which to perch, the detectives stood either side of the kitchen window – fully open and venting the pungent steam from over-cooked Brussels sprouts. Both men would have liked to vent some steam about their strange reception, but they could hear the woman moving around in the kitchen and said nothing.

A few minutes later, the officers heard a discussion in the kitchen.

"What? Police? What do they want? It's surely not about that vagrant who broke into the church hall, is it? I shall take back my every censure of the police, if so." Edwards' voice was perplexed, he was clearly not expecting any police contact, church hall break-in notwithstanding.

"I don't think so, reverend. Someone rang from Oxford, earlier, and said he'd be sending people to interview you about an incident there."

"Ohhh. That'll be about a tragic death at the

wake the other day – you remember I went to the funeral of a relative of mine. Actually, the man who died was also a relative, although not close. Where are they?"

"In the garden, reverend. I'll hold back your dinner until you've finished."

Edwards opened the back door. Haig and Kittow introduced themselves.

The curate looked to be just on the right side of thirty, of medium height, with fair wavy hair, and a supercilious expression.

"I hope this won't take too long," he started dismissively, making no attempt at the courtesies of greeting and introduction. "Mrs Simpkins has my lunch ready, and I have an appointment at church in an hour.

"Not too long at all, sir," replied Haig. "We're talking to everyone who was in the parlour at the wake on Tuesday, and saw the rector fall. I believe all the others were locals, and you seem to be the only one from out of county. We had to come to London for something else, so the chief inspector diverted us to see you – two birds with one stone, as he put it."

"I really can't help you," said Edwards testily. "What on earth can you possibly want to ask me?"

"We need to know how you knew the deceased, and also what happened when you were with the rector before he collapsed."

"Well, I'm related to the Hardwickes, of course – that's why I was invited to the funeral. The late Mrs Hardwicke came from a rather obscure branch of my family. I've lunched at the manor two or three times.

"In some way, I was also distantly related to Simeon Watson, although I'd never met him before. I didn't know a single person in the parlour, and I joined his group because, as a fellow cleric, I thought we might have something in common.

"Not so, as it turned out. He hardly stopped talking, and most of it was arrant nonsense. Apart from him, there were a couple of servants there – Hardwicke was ridiculously democratic in his guest list. Also, a beery sort of man who was a publican, I gathered. A desperately dull lawyer, and a doddery old soldier who looked and sounded as though he'd served at Waterloo, were also in the group.

"Hardwicke joined us for a few minutes. Said something about Beth having no money. I'm sure that wasn't true, as her father was quite well-off – he was in trade. But Hardwicke can be pretty devious, and he talks a lot of rubbish, too.

"Anyway, I just saw Watson fall and start thrashing and writhing. Someone went for a doctor, and then an overbearing pair of old codgers who'd been commandeering the wine as if they owned it, ordered us all to leave the room."

"You didnae have any sort of grudge against Mr Watson yourself, sir?" asked Haig.

"Don't be ridiculous, man; how could I? I'd never met him before. Even on my previous visits to the manor I never came across him."

"And you didnae happen to see anyone add anything to Mr Watson's food or drink?"

"Certainly not. I think you lot have vivid imaginations. You're making a song and dance about nothing. He just ate something that was off, probably. Got botulism or listeriosis, or something like that."

Haig didn't think it worthwhile prolonging the interview to explain about the strychnine, as the curate had no discernible link to the case, much less a motive, and was clearly itching to start his lunch.

The two officers took their leave, Edwards again not attempting to shake hands.

"Blimey, sarge," said Kittow when they were back in the car, "what a rum pair. I didn't take to them at all – him even less so than her!"

"Aye. I don't think you were there when the colonel said Edwards was a snob. And how right he was – *'in trade'* indeed!"

The two men found a café in nearby Stratford before starting back to Mistram, this time Haig taking the wheel.

****

Bryce and Jarvis, each having satisfied his 'inner man', began the journey to Major Hick's house. Jarvis said the village was about nine miles out of town, in the opposite direction to Mistram, but that he didn't know where the house was.

Bryce, now comfortable with Jarvis's driving, relaxed and enjoyed the countryside. Quite soon, the car entered a pretty village. Bryce spotted a yokel leaning against a five-bar gate. The man was almost a caricature version of the type – wearing a dirty-white smock, sucking on a straw, and with his trousers tied off with string in the manner used to contain ferrets. Bryce told Jarvis to stop. Winding down his window, he asked the man for directions to White Peacocks. To the DCI's surprise, the man answered succinctly and in an educated voice.

"Two hundred yards down this street, next turning on the left, which is a cul-de-sac, and you'll see the house ahead of you."

Bryce looked at the man again, very carefully. The man stared back, without any change of expression, although the DCI thought he might have detected the tiniest indication of amusement. Based on that perception, he gave his thanks but didn't offer the shilling that he had ready in his hand.

Following the instructions, Jarvis found that there was a short drive from the road up to the house, with space for at least three cars to park. The house itself wasn't huge – perhaps five bedrooms plus some second-floor rooms – but very attractive, with what might be termed a 'cottage garden' to the front.

Original Queen Anne style, thought Bryce, probably around two hundred and fifty years old. He assumed Hicks must have inherited the property together with money to keep it up, as the salary of a major could never have been sufficient to buy this place.

The two officers got out of the car, and were walking towards the front when they were interrupted by a shout, and a man who could only be Hicks emerged around the far corner of the house.

"'Morning sergeant," he called. "And you must be Chief Inspector Bryce," he added as he reached them, shaking hands.

"Come and sit down in my den," he said, leading them around to a back garden which looked to be a good acre in size. About halfway down, and tucked to one side, was a shed, equipped with a veranda on which were placed three Lloyd Loom chairs. These, Bryce was surprised to note, were 'Airship' models, huge and very comfortable looking. He had seen them in Lusty's pre-war catalogue, but never expected to sit in one.

"What about some refreshments, gentlemen?" Hicks asked. Both officers accepted the suggestion of tea, and the major rang a large handbell which was standing on a table beside the chairs.

Bryce looked around the spartan but snug little cabin with great interest. It was clearly a comfortable bolt hole, with plenty of evidence on the bookshelves that the major enjoyed military history.

"I spend a lot of time out here in good weather," explained Hicks. "Even in a rainstorm I like to sit here on the verandah, as long as it's not too cold. I've even got a bit of plumbing installed, so I can stay here all day if I feel like it; all night too, if I pull out the put-you-up over there." The major pointed to a curtained off area to one side.

A young maid dressed in traditional uniform appeared. She bobbed a curtsey to the major, and another to the officers.

"Tea for three, please Hannah, and something edible, if cook has anything."

The girl smiled, bobbed again, and left.

"Now, gentlemen," said Hicks, "how can I help you? You were very cagey this morning on the telephone, chief inspector."

"I take it you haven't heard that the Reverend Watson died in hospital, major?"

"No, I haven't," replied Hicks in a surprised tone. "Didn't know the man well, and didn't much care for what I did know of him. But give him his due, he'd just done a decent job of burying Beth. Food poisoning, was it? He certainly didn't look too good when we all cleared out of the parlour."

"Actually, major, he was deliberately poisoned with a large dose of strychnine," said Bryce.

"The deuce he was!" said Hicks, clearly shocked. "Well, I can assure you that I didn't do it, and I have absolutely no idea who did. I'd met the rector at Hardwicke's place a few times over the years, but we were never on intimate terms. Matter of fact, I'm not sure that he and Hardwicke were really friends. I take it that all those of us in the parlour on Tuesday are potential suspects?"

"That's right, major, and we are talking to everyone who was in the room that afternoon.

"Give us a picture of the people in the parlour, if you would."

The major might have been getting on in years, but like his contemporary Hardwicke, he retained all his faculties. Indeed, he would have been highly offended had he heard of Edwards' dismissive comment. Without needing any time to think he instantly rattled off those present:

"There was a youngish farmer, a gardener, the local publican, the land agent, a maid, and Hardwicke's solicitor. I'd never met the first three before. I'd met Dauntsey and McKay a few times at dinner, and of course I'd seen the maid, Doreen, often enough, although this was the first time I'd really spoken to her. Nice girl – very shy in that gathering, though.

"Then Watson joined us – can't say he lightened the atmosphere. He did a fine job with the funeral and interment, but in the parlour he just seemed odd. Rude, really, towards some of the guests.

"He'd not been there many minutes when another padre came along. Said he was related to Beth in some way. Didn't say a lot after that.

It seemed nobody, including Watson who was also allegedly related to him somehow, knew this curate fellow at all.

"Anyway, there was the desultory kind of conversation you get at that sort of sad gathering. You know how it is; so many subjects are off-limits, and people don't really have a lot to say to one another, but find something to say just the same. That went on for about half an hour.

"At one point, Watson sent the maid to fetch him some wine – she was a guest at the time, so that was out of order, I thought. Then he got one of the grandchildren to bring him some coffee.

"Just before that, Hardwicke had joined us for a few minutes, but he didn't say much. Basically just said 'hello' to us all. Explained how there was to be no formal reading of the will, and went off again to talk to other guests.

"A few minutes after drinking his coffee, the rector had his seizure and just dropped to the deck. We all left the room, and he was taken away in an ambulance. Soon after that I said 'goodbye' to Miles and Esther, and came home. That's it."

"Well, thanks for that, major. I can't say we came here with high hopes that you'd provide the solution, but we have to follow routine."

The maid returned with the refreshments, and Hicks busied himself sorting out the cups and plates. When that was done, Bryce apologised:

"I fear we are delaying you unnecessarily, major, because I think I've finished asking about the murder."

"Don't worry about that, chief inspector. I'm glad to have you here. I don't get that many visitors, so if you and the sergeant can spare the time I assure you that I can!"

"Well, in that case, I do have a couple of irrelevant questions for you while we drink our tea.

"We asked a man in the village for directions to your house. I thought he was a classic country yokel. But when he spoke he certainly didn't sound like one. Do you know him?"

Hicks nearly fell out of his chair, laughing.

"I do," he said. "You're quite correct in thinking he isn't a country bumpkin. That's the seventh Viscount Joyner – he lives at the hall and owns half of the village!"

"Glad I hung on to my shilling, then," smiled Bryce.

"Coals to Newcastle, that would have been," Hicks chortled. "The man owns hundreds of acres around here, plus another big estate in Scotland."

"Rather odd behaviour, though," said Bryce.

"Yes, he's what I would fondly call thoroughly eccentric. Highly intelligent, completely harmless, and probably very badly misunderstood by the medical profession, who seem to want to hook him up to those damned fangled electrodes from time to time." Hicks shook his head and shuddered, "Wouldn't allow those trick cyclists anywhere near me or any relation of mine."

"Another question, major, also not related to the case," said the DCI, patting the arms of his seat. "These chairs – there can't be many like this around. This was the type used in the R100 airship, wasn't it?"

"That's right!" confirmed the major, clearly delighted that the DCI had some knowledge and interest in his furniture. "But they were also popular with fighter pilots during the war – the men could sit comfortably in their full flying kit while waiting for the order to 'scramble'. A couple of years ago one of the RAF airfields in Suffolk was closed, and there was a sale of all sorts of surplus stuff. I happened to be in the area at the time, and went along to the auction – out of curiosity, really. Half a dozen of these were included. I bought three, and I was sorry to see there were hardly any other bids."

"A good buy, I think, major."

Their tea drunk, Bryce thanked the old soldier, and stood up. "We'll leave you in peace now," he added.

Hicks escorted the two men to their car, and gave a half-salute as they drove away.

"Before you ask, sir; no, I don't see him as a murderer. I met him once when he was visiting Mistram. Lovely man. The colonel told me that the two of them were at the Royal Military College together – that would have been about a year or two before the old Queen died. They were both badly wounded in the Great War, one on the Somme and the other at 'Wipers'."

"I feel the same way, sergeant, I can't see him poisoning anyone. But, as he's about the only person we've seen who doesn't have a grudge against the rector, in a contrary sort of way perhaps we should follow the examples in popular fiction and suspect him even more than those with motives!

"The next person on my list is Anderson, at New Farm. I've arranged to see him at between three and four o'clock."

They made good time, and Jarvis drew the car to a halt outside a modest farmhouse. Bryce, assessing the exterior, thought the 'new' probably meant it was built in the early twentieth century, rather than in the eighteenth or nineteenth.

"I think this time, sergeant, it might be more tactful if I see Mr Anderson alone," said Bryce. Jarvis nodded understandingly.

The DCI got out of the car and approached the front door. It was opened before he could knock, and he found himself facing a well-built man in his thirties or early forties. The mid October weather was distinctly cool, but the farmer had his shirtsleeves tightly rolled up over muscular and hirsute arms. Thick leather braces supported muddied trousers, which disappeared into the tops of even muddier wellingtons. He looked a most capable 'son of the soil'.

"Good afternoon, Mr Anderson. I'm DCI

Bryce."

Anderson shook the DCI's offered hand and invited him into a small room equipped with an old desk and a couple of battered chairs. Seed and farming catalogues and leaflets were stacked around the room, with more papers and Government notices and directives pinned to two large notice boards.

"Sit down, chief inspector."

Anderson was quick to appreciate that Bryce had come alone to the house. "Very considerate of you, leaving Sergeant Jarvis in the car. I'm assuming you've heard about my marriage troubles, and no doubt Jarvis knows all about them too; but it's still easier to talk to one person, especially a stranger."

"I thought so," replied Bryce. "Just give me a very brief outline of what happened, please."

"I don't know exactly when it started. Perhaps five or six months ago. Vicky started to go round to the rectory more and more. Now she wasn't a friend of Mrs Ellis, nor of Alice, either. To start with I just thought she had some sort of spiritual problem – seemed a bit odd, but she refused to talk about it with me. I didn't have any suspicions to start with. Of course, you sort of automatically trust a man of the cloth, don't you? And he was years older than her, too."

"But after a few weeks, I did start to get properly suspicious, so I tackled her about it, head on. To begin with, she tried to lie her way past my questions, but in the end she admitted to having an affair. Said she was going to live with the rector.

"I shouted at her, and she shouted back. I'd never laid a hand on her in anger before, and if anyone had told me that I'd ever want to do it, I wouldn't have believed them. But I felt like it that day." Anderson looked down at his big hands on the desk, utterly wretched as he re-lived the episode.

"Anyway, I drove off right away and went to the rectory. By chance, Watson came to the door himself. I told him I knew what he was doing with Vicky, and he didn't deny it.

"I nearly attacked him with my fists. He was a big man, but a lot older than me and not fit – I could have handled him easily. But I'm not stupid, chief inspector, and I knew that would've put me in the wrong, and probably in prison. I'm only a tenant farmer, and he was the high-and-mighty priest – and from a county family. The likes of me can't expect to go up against that sort and win. I just told him that he was welcome to her, and she could move into the rectory straight away.

"Well, he gave me a funny look. 'You are misinformed,' he said. 'We had our fun, but there's nothing more to it than that. I can't have someone else's wife living here with me. It's finished now.'

"I told him exactly what I thought of him, and he just stood there sort of smirking. In the end I went home. I told Vicky what he'd said, but she didn't believe me. I said that I didn't care either way, and that she had to move out the next day. Told her I didn't want to see her again. If he wouldn't take her in, I said she'd better go back to her mother. We don't have children. Never thought the day would come when I'd be glad about that."

Anderson sat very still. Bryce formed the impression of a decent man who had suffered the worst kind of betrayal. He felt extremely sorry for the farmer.

After a long sigh, Anderson said:

"I don't know whether or not she went to the rectory the next day, but she didn't move in there, that's for sure. She's at her mother's and she's already written to me twice pleading for forgiveness, begging me to take her back. I've not replied as yet; I'm not sure what to do." Anderson looked even more dejected and miserable now.

"In other circumstances it's the sort of thing I might talk over with a priest who knew us both, chief inspector, but that's a route not open to me now. I don't doubt the colonel knows about this by now; I've a great respect for him, and maybe he'll talk through this with me."

"I think that's a very good idea, Mr Anderson," agreed Bryce. "I'm sure he'll listen sympathetically and talk through your choices, if that's what you'd like. After that, you may feel a lot better about reaching a decision.

"Obviously, I'm trying to find a motive for this murder, Mr Anderson. You probably know that there are several people in this parish with reasons to dislike the late rector, and you'll appreciate that your reason is better than most. You might have decided to stay calm initially, perhaps thinking that revenge is a dish best served cold, as the saying goes, and that you would settle the score later."

Anderson sat silently again, staring at his hands. Then, raising his head and holding Bryce's gaze, he said:

"I'm aware that a few other people had their reasons. But I realise that my quarrel probably puts me ahead of anyone else. So yes, I can see how it looks bad for me.

"But I didn't do it. I didn't get any poison, and I wouldn't even know how to get some. I don't approve of murder anyway. Frankly, I was planning how I might bring him down from his lofty perch with words, perhaps working together with some of his other victims. We might get a petition, and present it to the Bishop, for instance. Or get the Press interested. I'll admit I wanted my own back – but I never even considered killing him." Anderson shook his head and stared down at his desk. Giving a bitter little half-laugh he said, "Just didn't even cross my mind to finish him off."

Looking up again, the farmer offered: "There's something else a bit in my favour, though. I was one of the first to go into that parlour room on Tuesday, with Mr Dauntsey. I was right up at the far end. Several more people joined us. Watson was almost last to arrive. Now, I was amazed that he had the nerve to come and join a group with several people he knew he'd wronged and upset. He could and should have gone into one of the other rooms. He was just being provocative, I have no doubt.

"But the point is that there was absolutely no way I could have foreseen that he would come along. So even if I'd somehow obtained poison, there was no reason to believe that he'd have come near enough to me to let me administer it."

Bryce nodded. The farmer's motive was by far the best on offer, but instinct and experience were telling him that Anderson was not the killer. He stood up, "All right Mr Anderson, thank you. At some point you'll need to make a formal statement, but at this stage we haven't asked anyone to do that.

"Assuming to can't think of anything more to tell me, I'll go. I still have another witness to see today."

The DCI returned to the car.

"Back to the manor, please, Jarvis. I can tell you that interview wasn't very enlightening. I need to see the gardener Bixby now. Do you know him?"

"Yes, sir; nice honest lad. His father also works on the estate, he's a gamekeeper under Waites. His grandfather used to be a gamekeeper too. Young Tony loves gardening though, and someone must have told the colonel, because he offered the boy a job. Keeping must be in his blood, though, and maybe Tony'll change jobs when Waites retires. But I know he's very happy where he is."

"Let's get back to the manor and find him. I'd like to get that interview done before the others get back from London. However, I really don't have any other task for you today, sergeant, so when you've dropped me off you can disappear until tomorrow morning. Thanks for ferrying me about today. Come to the Dog at eight thirty again tomorrow morning."

CHAPTER 16

A footman answered the doorbell, and admitted Bryce. Miles Hardwicke happened to be passing, and stopped to talk to his friend.

"I know you can't give me any detail, Philip, but are you anywhere near cracking this yet?"

"Can't say that I am, Miles. You know as well as I do who the principal suspects are, and so far I've not been able to eliminate any of them with any certainty. Apart from Isla, perhaps," he added with a smile.

"I'd certainly be jolly concerned if she knew how to obtain strychnine," said her father with a laugh as the two walked towards the study. "But seriously, I don't envy you the task of filtering out the guilty party. From what Angie has said, the group around Simeon was quite close together, and unless someone actually saw something…

"I'm not interfering, of course, but have you thought of the possibility of a conspiracy between two or more of them?"

"Yes, but it's not a promising avenue of enquiry, simply because most of the motives are weak. If there's insufficient to motivate one person to act, they're unlikely to bother looking for someone else to team up with."

"Fair enough; I'll let you get on," said Miles, as Bryce prepared to enter the study.

"I don't suppose you know where I can find Bixby – he's the last of the group that I need to see?" asked the DCI, before opening the door.

"Matter of fact, yes. As I came downstairs a few minutes ago, I saw him through the half-landing window. He was on his knees in the herb garden. You can go out through the scullery door, turn left, and you should see him; or I'll have him sent to you."

Instead of going into the study as he had intended, Bryce followed his friend's instructions and went to find Bixby himself. Passing through the servants' hall, he encountered the cook, talking with a smart-looking woman whom he hadn't seen before.

"Good afternoon, Mrs Jeff. Would I be right in thinking you are Mrs Walters?" he asked the other.

"Quite right – and I guess I'd be right in thinking you are Chief Inspector Bryce," she smiled.

"For my sins, yes. Nice to meet you, Mrs Walters. I hear that you two ladies did wonders preparing for the wake – such a shame the rector's death cast a pall over your efforts. I'm actually on my way into the garden, if you would excuse my using your room as a shortcut."

The DCI passed through the scullery and out into the kitchen garden. Following Miles' instructions, he came to the herb garden.

His approach was spotted, and the man stood up. Tall and copper-haired, aged perhaps twenty-five, he somehow didn't look like a gardener – certainly not one in the Mr McGregor mould.

Bryce held out his hand. The young man hesitated, wiped his dirty hand on his trousers, looked at it again, and showed his palm to Bryce before saying "I don't really recommend it, sir."

"Very considerate, thank you," remarked the DCI. "I'm Chief Inspector Bryce, and I assume you are Anthony Bixby?"

"That's right, sir, and you want to ask about what happened on Tuesday?"

"Yes, if you can spare ten minutes or so. Let's go and sit over there."

The two walked a few yards to where a long wooden seat had been installed beside a glasshouse.

"Doreen says you managed to get her to tell you a few things about the rector. I suppose it don't look good, me having an argument with the man and moaning about him in the Dog."

"Actually, Mr Bixby, she didn't tell us about your spat with the rector. We picked that up from other people. And what she did tell us about him has also been confirmed by others. You have nothing to reproach her for.

"But just tell me about you and the rector."

"Well, sir, about a week ago we – me and Doreen – went to the rectory to ask about getting married. Alice showed us into a room and told us to wait. A few minutes later Mr Watson come in. Didn't even ask us to sit down, and he was very rude. He said 'I know you want to marry, and I can't stop you doing that, but I can stop you using my church. You aren't churchgoers, and the church isn't there just for when you fancy using it'.

"It's true that Doreen and me haven't gone to church since we left Sunday school years ago – 'cept for a couple of funerals and someone else's wedding. And I can understand his position, really. But it was the nasty way he said it that made me cross. And he made Doreen cry, so I wasn't happy. Anyway, that was that, and we left straight away.

"At the wake, Doreen went into church for the service, 'cos she had to go back before the burial. I wouldn't go in, and just walked around the churchyard for a bit. I spoke to Mr Dauntsey, who hadn't gone in either for some reason. Then I watched the burial. The colonel had invited everyone back to the manor, so I went too. In the house, Doreen come up to me and said she didn't have any jobs and could stay with me. We went to get some food. Young Mrs Hardwicke was very nice, like she always is. Gave us each a plate and spoke to us for a bit. Once it got more crowded where the food was, we went through to the next room, and stood with Mr Dauntsey and Mr Anderson and Mr Eccles, and a couple of other people I didn't know.

"Then the rector come and joined us. Well, Doreen and me, we weren't happy, but there wasn't much we could do about it. He didn't speak to us anyway, 'cept once when he told Doreen to fetch him some wine.

"Then later he sort of started moaning, and fell to the floor and almost immediately the old army gentlemen cleared us all out of the room.

"That's all I can tell you, sir."

"Just confirm something else for me, please. You didn't say, but I understand the colonel joined the group for a short while. Also, someone brought him some coffee. Now, just put these things in order, please. Doreen fetching the wine, the coffee, the colonel coming and going, the rector collapsing."

"That's easy, sir. Wine first; then the colonel came and went; then Miss Isla brought the coffee; then he collapsed. Maybe ten minutes from her bringing the coffee to him going down."

"Good, thank you. And I assume that you didn't notice anyone interfering with any of the rector's food or drink?"

"No, I certainly didn't, sir."

"All right, thank you. In fairness to you and Doreen, I hardly think that his refusal to marry you in what he called 'his' church would cause you to kill him. If you'd punched him on the nose it might have been understandable, although it still wouldn't have been justified. Now, until I actually charge someone with murder, and he or she is convicted by a jury, I have to keep an open mind. But if it helps, you can tell your fiancée that I don't seriously suspect either of you."

"Thank you for that, sir; much obliged."

Bryce made his way back thorough the house and sat down in the study to think. He mentally reviewed each of the suspects who had some sort of disagreement with Watson. Nothing seemed to elevate any one of these disputes – apart from Anderson's – to something which might be produced in court as a motive. Far from it, in fact.

Undoubtedly Anderson had made a fair point about not expecting to be near the rector. However, that same potential defence might equally apply to most, if not all, of the others. The possibility that the rector may well have arrived by happenstance to stand near his assailant in the parlour, didn't get around the fact that the murderer could easily have gone to find him in another room, if Watson hadn't gone into the parlour.

Bryce then considered those who, as far as he knew, had no such dispute. Again, he was no further forward. Also, even if some sort of more likely motive should emerge, proving that a particular individual introduced the poison to the dead man would be practically impossible.

Of course, they might be very lucky, and be able to prove that a particular individual purchased strychnine, but he thought that would be a long shot. Nevertheless, in the absence of any other line of investigation, he decided to institute a trawl around the chemists within a fifteen-mile radius or so; certainly in the local town, and even as far as Oxford itself.

Since the 1868 Pharmacy Act, sale of certain drugs – including strychnine – had been restricted, and a 'poison register' showing any such purchase had to be kept by pharmacists. Bryce decided to send Kittow, and perhaps Jarvis, out in the morning to inspect registers, and told himself that he should have put this exercise higher up his priority list.

He was still sitting, brooding over the lack of progress and the possibility that this might be the first case he didn't solve, when Haig and Kittow returned.

"Welcome back," he said. "I have absolutely nothing from today's exercise, so I hope you two have some better news?"

Both men shook their heads.

"Sorry, sir, nothing from us – apart from the fact that you'd have to go on a long day's march before you met two ruder people than Edwards and his landlady," said Haig.

Bryce laughed. "Alas, we're looking for something a bit more indictable than rudeness, sergeant. Oh well, ring the bell, will you. Let's send for some tea, and then we'll exchange reports."

Ten minutes later, when the rigmarole with the trays had been completed and each man had a cup of tea and some sort of oat biscuit in front of him, Bryce told Haig to kick off.

Haig was now getting very good at presenting an oral report. He told the DCI first about Hendon, and handed over the note regarding the rector's palate.

"In all honesty, I didn't expect much from my query," said Bryce, "and although it's good of them to do a bit more investigation, I'm still not expecting anything useful. But go on."

Haig moved on to the Ilford visit, referring to his pocketbook, where he had made a lot of notes while sitting in the car outside Edwards' lodging before they drove off. He gave an almost verbatim account of what had been said.

On completion, he looked up and said:

"The colonel said he was snobbish, and he is. He gave the impression that not only was the late Beth Hardwicke from an inferior branch of his family, but that marrying the colonel had taken her even further downhill.

"But if you remember, sir, the colonel also said the man was obsequious, and that he agreed with everything anyone said. No sign of that today, and in fact Edwards said that the colonel often talked rubbish, and was devious.

"Still, perhaps previously he'd been hoping

for a legacy from Mrs Beth, and now he'd found out there was no legacy, he no longer needed to grovel. How did you and Jarvis get on, sir?"

"We saw Dauntsey, McKay, and Hicks. And I've seen Anderson and Bixby by myself."

Bryce ran through the main points of the five interviews.

"Anderson has by far the most compelling motive. I couldn't blame anyone for wanting some sort of revenge on the man who made him a cuckold. And he has admitted as much, although he says through lawful means. I have to say I'm inclined to believe him.

"I feel dreadfully stuck on this one. I'm sorry, Kittow; if you were expecting a swift solution, and then back to London, I fear you're out of luck."

"Not a problem for me, sir. As I said last night, a few more weeks staying at the Dog and Partridge isn't exactly penal servitude," replied the young DC with a laugh. "But I do want this solved, sir," he added quickly, worried that he might have given the wrong impression.

The three officers sat quietly, drinking the last of their tea, and thinking. Five minutes passed, when Bryce suddenly sat up straight and faced Haig.

"Tell me again what was said by Edwards and his landlady when he arrived back at his digs – as exactly as you can."

Haig took out his pocketbook again, and

repeated what he had said earlier, turning to check whether Kittow's recollection of the overheard conversation matched his own.

"A glimmer of hope, gentlemen – which may well be dashed, but we must pursue it," said Bryce when Kittow had emphatically confirmed Haig's account. He rose and pressed the bell push.

To Feeke, who came in response, he said, "My compliments to the colonel, if he's around. I'd appreciate it if he could spare me a few minutes. If it's more convenient, I'll go to him, of course."

Within five minutes, the colonel arrived in the study. As before, Kittow went to sit in the window.

"A quick question, colonel. After the news of the rector's death arrived here on Tuesday evening, did you contact anyone to pass on that information? I know you didn't inform Major Hicks, because he didn't even know Watson was dead until I told him today. But did you tell anyone else?"

"No, I didn't. Not a soul. Oh, apart from Mrs Ellis, but the hospital had already informed her. I didn't really think to speak to anyone else. Why do you ask?"

"I'll answer that in a moment, colonel, but first a supplementary question: would your immediate family members have taken it upon themselves to contact anyone?"

"I'm certain not. However, they're all in the drawing room. Go along there now and ask them yourself. I'll stay here so as not to give them a hint as to what to say!"

Bryce got up without a word, and quickly covered the distance to the drawing room. He knocked and went in.

"Oh lord, I hope you haven't come to tell us you've arrested father," said Esther.

"Certainly not; what a notion," said Bryce. "No, at his suggestion I've come to pose a question to all of you.

"After Jarvis brought the news of the rector's death here on Tuesday evening, did any one of you contact anyone else to inform him or her about it – then, or at any time since?"

All four shook their heads, and looked puzzled by the question.

Miles spoke first. "If anyone was going to do that, it would be father," he said, "and I assume he's told you he did no such thing."

"Yes, he has. So, to be absolutely clear, none of you contacted the Reverend Edwards in London, between Tuesday evening and this morning?"

There was a general shaking of heads, and all four gave a clear 'no'.

"Thank you," said Bryce. "Please don't draw any conclusions from this!"

He returned to the study, where the colonel and Yard officers were talking about cricket.

"Finally, we have possible glimmer of light, gentlemen. Colonel, when my colleagues spoke to Mr Edwards in Ilford this morning, it seemed that he already knew that Watson was dead. This matter hasn't even reached the local newspapers yet, let alone the nationals.

"So, given that it seems nobody here told him, how did he know?"

There was a silence which Haig broke:

"But he hadn't even met Mr Watson before, sir. Why would he want to kill a man he didnae even know?"

"That's right," said Hardwicke. "Certainly, to my knowledge they didn't know each other, although they were very distantly related."

"I'll tentatively propose a theory about that." said Bryce. "You said, colonel, that on Edwards' previous visits he was particularly obsequious, agreeing with your every word. 'Oily', I think was your description of him. Yet when he saw my officers this morning, he displayed nothing of that manner. On the contrary, he was positively confrontational. Also, he said that you – please forgive me – are devious and talk rubbish."

Hardwicke growled.

"Now from that," continued Bryce, "I deduce that when he was here before it was imperative that he should get into your good books – ingratiate himself, in fact.

"When reporting this morning's conversation, Sergeant Haig here put forward a theory as to why Edwards' attitude changed. I understand that it was widely known for some months that your late wife was seriously ill, and

Haig thought that he might have been hoping that she would leave him something. When you announced that there were no legacies, he didn't need to dissimulate any more.

"That theory has some merit, but I don't think it's the correct one. First of all, I think Edwards was caught completely off-guard when my men arrived at his lodgings. It's clear from what Haig and Kittow heard him say to his housekeeper that she hadn't contacted him beforehand to warn him of their visit. Indeed, she told me on the telephone that she would wait until he returned for lunch.

"Anyway, she wasn't told of Watson's death, nor why we wanted to interview her lodger.

"Edwards was surprised into making two errors. The first was showing that he knew that Watson was dead. He could only be aware of that if he knew that the man had taken a fatal dose of poison.

"The second, I think, was almost as stupid. By making a couple of cutting and unflattering remarks about you, colonel, he didn't take into account the possibility – admittedly small – that you might get to hear about what he had said. If my own theory is right, that would have been fatal as far as his plan was concerned."

Hardwicke suddenly took a sharp intake of breath and slapped the palms of his hands down on the arms of his chair. "Of course!" he cried, "how stupid of me not to see it before, chief inspector. You've evidently worked out what I should have seen from the very first time he came here. Do tell your colleagues – you deserve the credit."

Bryce looked embarrassed but began his explanation, "There are three key points. The first two were known to us: that Mr Edwards is an ordained priest; and that he is currently posted to a lowly appointment in a parish which is probably not to his liking – being, as all of you have said, a snob of the first order.

"We drew no conclusions from those – and initially there was no reason to do so.

"However, a few minutes ago when we realised about his premature knowledge of the rector's death, I considered those again. It was only then that the third and most crucial point came to my mind.

"I assume, colonel, that you hold the advowson for this living?"

"Absolutely right, Bryce, well done."

Seeing Haig and Kittow looking lost, the DCI explained. "An advowson gives a patron, in this case the colonel here, the right to present a priest to the bishop for appointment – effectively to put his own nominee into the rectory. It's a very ancient right.

"You actually told us yesterday, colonel, but again I didn't draw any conclusions from it, that this living is an unusually good one. I don't suppose you ever mentioned that in Edwards' hearing, but it probably wouldn't have been too hard to find it out.

"In any case, though, for a man of his ilk, being the incumbent here in these peaceful and beautiful surroundings would certainly have been far more appealing than a curacy in east London, regardless of the financial value."

"You are one hundred percent correct," said Hardwicke. "I could kick myself for not seeing through him a year ago.

"The fact is that even if I'd thought Edwards would make a better rector, and even though I didn't always see eye to eye with Watson, I had no power to sack the man. Once appointed, only the bishop can remove him, and only then for cause, after due process. As Watson was unlikely to be made a bishop, he might expect to stay here into his nineties – as in fact the previous incumbent did. Edwards' only hope of gaining the living was to sweeten me up, and to eliminate his fellow cleric."

Bryce nodded. "Yes, I believe you've assessed Edwards' thinking very accurately. Actually, colonel, you gave me another clue yesterday. You said that you didn't have the *power* to overrule the rector. I think most people, without any influence at all in the matter, would speak instead of *attempting* to change his mind. Only someone who actually held some authority – in your case effectively the power to appoint a candidate – would even mention overruling him."

CHAPTER 17

There was a silence in the room, as the four men contemplated the matter. Hardwicke and Kittow were having the same thought. How many cases had there been in modern times where an English priest committed murder – and was there any precedent for one priest to kill another?

The minds of Bryce and Haig were also in synchronism. Each was thinking that although the solution was almost certainly correct, proof was currently wanting. Bryce put this thought into words.

"It's up to us to prove this now," he said. "At present, there isn't enough to go to court with.

"I could certainly arrest him, but unless he broke down almost straight away, I couldn't risk charging him yet.

"This is what we'll do. Time may be of the essence here – and we may already be too late. Sergeant, you and Kittow take the car and go back to London now. Find a magistrate this evening, swear out an information, and ask for a warrant to search Edwards' lodgings. I hardly think he'd leave any evidence in his church, and I'm not too sure about a warrant for that anyway.

"Then, assuming you get a warrant, go straight round to his lodgings. Initially, don't mention the warrant. Get a statement from his landlady, clearly repeating what Edwards said this morning about your visit being because his relation was dead. Obviously, he shouldn't be within earshot when you talk to her – take her out to the car if he's around.

"When you've got the statement from her, execute the warrant straight away. If he is out, so much the better, but even if he is home I doubt if he'll kick up much of a fuss. If he does, then arrest him on my authority, on suspicion of murder – lock him up at the nearest nick and I'll come and talk to him tomorrow. If we're really lucky, he'll still have something incriminating in his room.

"If you finish before closing time, ring me at the Dog and Partridge to report. Otherwise, leave a message for me at the Yard.

"When you've done the search, go home, both of you – whether or not you find anything, and whether or not you've had to arrest him.

"The next step will be to check the poison registers in every pharmacy in and around Ilford. Again, we may be lucky. As you know, strychnine may only be sold by a qualified pharmacist, and only to someone he knows personally – or to an intermediary who is known to both of them. There's just a chance that this was bought from one of his parishioners.

"So, make a start on the pharmacies in the morning. I'll try to get a list. Or I dare say the local station can give you names and locations – from the electoral roll, perhaps. Start with ones closest to him, and work outwards.

"You'll have noticed that I'm leaving all this to you two. I could make the excuse that I need to spend this evening writing what is going to be a lengthy report. Or that I'm giving you some valuable experience. Both would be perfectly true.

"Or I could come clean, and admit that after doing five interviews today to your one, I'm very tired!

"Anyway, drop me off at the Dog on your way back, please. I'll get Jarvis to bring me to the city tomorrow.

"Sticking my neck out here, I'm feeling confident we have a result, which means you shouldn't need to come back. So pick up your bags from the inn."

Hardwicke had been listening to these instructions with keen interest.

"My children and their spouses must be itching with curiosity, following your earlier question. And I'm not sure I can withstand the pressure that they'll probably apply. Is it in order for me to pass on this information about Edwards?" he asked.

"Yes; with the obvious proviso that it goes no further before tomorrow," replied Bryce. "I won't come to say goodbye, but you might just point out to Angie that she has no chance of a Treasury brief on this one – when conducting a case, she can't alternate between the prosecutor's table and the witness box!"

With handshakes all round, the officers left. In the car, Bryce remembered his promise.

"Stop at the church on the way, Kittow," he said to the young DC. "You can take a few minutes to look at the lych gate; a slight diversion like that won't change anything."

At the inn, Bryce explained that although he was staying, his colleagues were leaving, but that he was sure Superintendent Denton would honour the original arrangement as far as payment was concerned. Haig and Kittow collected their things, and left for London.

Bryce shut himself in the little booth between the bars, which contained the telephone.

First, he called Scotland Yard, and spoke to his secretary.

"Find a detective constable, Mrs Finlay, and instruct him to produce a list of pharmacies within a three-mile radius of Ilford. I don't care how he does it, but if he hurries, the easiest way would be to call the Pharmaceutical Society before they go home, and get the information from them. If that fails, he'll have to call the Ilford police station, and see if someone there can help.

"I've no idea how many chemists there will be – I guess at least twenty. But I want that list, names and addresses, hand delivered to Sergeant Haig's house by ten o'clock tonight.

"I expect to be in the office myself late in the morning tomorrow."

Next he called Veronica, telling her – to her surprise and delight – that he expected to be home the following evening.

He then placed a quick call to Fiona Haig, advising her that Alex would be back later that evening. She too was pleased. As Kittow lived with his parents and had no telephone, Bryce didn't think a further telegram would be justified.

Finally, he called Superintendent Denton, explaining that although he didn't want to name names over the telephone, it was likely that the investigation would be finished the following day. He promised to call then, with an update. Denton, who had expected that the Yard men would be around for a lot longer, was also delighted, and didn't demur when the DCI asked for Sergeant Jarvis to take him back to London.

His calls made, the DCI asked Eccles if he might use the dining room as an office. This arrangement agreed, he took out a new foolscap writing pad, and began his draft report. Mrs Eccles supplied him with tea, a requisite fuel for all police paperwork.

Bryce went out for an hour's brisk walk before dinner, returning to enjoy a solitary meal of cottage pie. He was just draining the last of his coffee when Eccles came in to say that there was a telephone call.

"Haig here, sir," he heard. "I got the warrant, no problem. When we got to his diggings, Edwards was out. Mrs Simpkins, the landlady, made the statement exactly as you wanted.

"I'd just explained the warrant to her when Edwards came home. He kicked up a proper stink. He has the whole of the first floor – tried to stop us getting into his rooms.

"He was being so difficult that I arrested him. No idea if I've done the right thing, sir, but I've only arrested him for obstructing a police officer. No mention of suspicion of murder. He's not been charged, but Ilford is holding him overnight.

"Anyway, the bad news is that we found absolutely nothing incriminating when we went back in the house. We even searched the garden shed, but nothing suspicious there either. Sorry, sir."

"Can't be helped, sergeant. And it was a good idea to use the obstruction offence. I'll come and see him sometime tomorrow.

"I've got the list of chemists around the Ilford area; thanks, sir. It'll make the job much easier in the morning."

"Yes, I hoped it would. I'll look into the Yard around eleven tomorrow morning. Give me a call there if you have any success."

****

The following morning, Sergeant Jarvis took Bryce to London, the DCI giving directions. Jarvis was astounded to learn that the case appeared to be closed, and disappointed that his own involvement was now over.

Back in his own office, Bryce gave his secretary his draft report to type. He called down to thank DC Spencer for doing a good job with the list of chemists, and then busied himself prioritising the accumulation of paperwork in his in-tray. Half an hour later, his telephone rang.

"DC Kittow here, sir," came an excited voice. "We've got him!

"Only the fourth place we tried. Edwards bought strychnine sulphate there three days ago. He told the chemist that his church was plagued with rats. The chemist knew Edwards by sight, and knew what he did, but didn't actually know him personally; and so technically didn't comply with the law. Anyway, sir, Edwards was wearing his dog collar, and signed the register in his own name. Sergeant Haig is just taking the chemist's statement now.

"We'll be off again soon, to check at the vicarage whether there's any truth in the rats story."

"Very well, done," said Bryce. "Good idea about the vicarage too. Since nobody saw Edwards administer the poison, and you've found no evidence at his lodgings, we may need to do a belt-and-braces job on this one, and arrange an identification parade for the pharmacist to pick out Edwards. But hopefully that won't be necessary.

"Right, I'm coming to Ilford now. When you've seen the vicar, go to the station and I'll see you there."

Bryce put his head through the door of the secretaries' room.

"Mrs Finlay, please call the 'J' Division DDI. Tell him I have a murder suspect at Ilford police station. Just a courtesy call to say that I'm working in his patch – you can tell him that the murder was in Oxfordshire, and isn't his problem."

Taking a car from the pool, Bryce drove out to Ilford. He found Haig and Kittow chatting to the custody sergeant.

"The Vicar says he's never seen any sign of any rodents in the church," said Haig. "We had to say why we asked, and he just snorted. Got the impression he doesn't think much of his curate."

"All very good, gentlemen."

Bryce turned to the custody sergeant:

"Has he given you any grief?"

"Not a peep out of him, sir, not since Sergeant Haig here left last night. Hasn't even asked for a solicitor. In your own time of course, sir, but room two is available now."

"Good, bring him along now."

The big sergeant disappeared, and the three

officers found room two. Haig and Kittow readied themselves to take detailed notes as the custody sergeant escorted Edwards into the room.

"Sit down, Mr Edwards," said Bryce, not offering to shake hands. "I'm Detective Chief Inspector Bryce. Caution him, sergeant."

Haig complied.

"You were arrested yesterday for obstruction of a police office in the execution of his duty."

"Ridiculous!" interjected the curate angrily. "They said they were going to search my rooms, and that was a gross infringement of my rights. What they expected to find I can't imagine. I shall be writing to the Commissioner, and to my Member of Parliament, about this."

"You are welcome to do that, of course; however, I think you may have another matter to concentrate on before you get around to that.

"First, I'll just point out that these officers were in possession of a magistrate's warrant to carry out the search, so they were acting completely lawfully, and you had no right to get in their way. That is why you were arrested. But I'm not concerned with that, and you won't be charged with obstructing them."

"I should think not, indeed," snapped Edwards rising to his feet, apparently thinking he was free to leave.

"Not just yet, Mr Edwards, I haven't quite finished. I simply meant that your obstruction was too trivial a matter for us to bother with. I want to talk to you about the death of the Reverend Simeon Watson, at Mistram Manor, on Tuesday of this week.

"You're perfectly entitled to stand and hear what I have to say," said Bryce calmly and pleasantly. "But we generally find people on your side of the table need to sit when accused of murder."

"I know nothing about that!" shouted Edwards. "Nothing at all!"

"Well, we shall have to see," replied Bryce. "But first, would you like to have a solicitor present, or are you content to carry on with this interview?"

Edwards glowered at him, his eyes darting around as he thought about the offer. Eventually, he sat down again.

"No – I don't need a solicitor. I've told you; I know nothing about Watson. And I don't know what your men expected to find in my rooms, but, as they must have seen, there wasn't anything to find anyway."

"Quite true," replied Bryce gently. "Now, you've been cautioned. "What did you do with the bottle of strychnine?"

Edwards spluttered and flapped his arms. "I don't know what you mean. I've never had any strychnine. This is an outrage – an utter outrage!"

"Well, others might say that it's rather more outrageous for Mr Watson to be poisoned."

Edwards said nothing, his expression – and his arms – now very still.

"Yesterday, these two officers came to interview you. I'll be perfectly candid – yours was just one of a number of routine interviews with people who were at the wake.

"But when you arrived at the house, and discovered that they were waiting, you told your landlady – in their hearing – that they had come to talk about the rector's death.

"Now, Mr Edwards, just how did you know that he was dead?"

"You're trying to trick me," blustered Edwards. "I obviously read it in the paper."

Haig leaned towards Edwards, making a show of turning over a fresh leaf in his notebook before saying "Aye, well it'd be grand if you just give me the name and edition of the paper right now. Bound to be fresh in your mind, I don't doubt, being so recent."

Edwards looked stunned for a moment, but recovered quickly, "I don't remember the name of the paper I read it in. And I'm sure Mrs Simpkins has lit the fires with it since then."

"I think you'll have to do better than that at some time in the future, Mr Edwards," said Bryce smoothly. In court, for example, if I were prosecuting I'd expect you to produce any newspaper which had reported this death before you spoke to Mrs Simpkins. As the sergeant has just demonstrated, you'll find that rather difficult."

Edwards was silent.

Bryce continued:

"And that won't be your only difficulty. You've been to Mistram two or three times recently, I believe?"

"Yes; why ever not? I'm a relation! Is everyone who visits relations a murderer?" Edwards was shouting more loudly and becoming agitated again.

"So I understand. But you are what, twenty-nine years old? Yet it seems you paid your first visit less than a year ago. Did you only just find out about these relations?"

Again, Edwards didn't answer.

"We are noting your non-responses. When did you learn that Colonel Hardwicke held the advowson for Mistram?"

"I expect I heard on one of my visits."

"Oh, really? Bryce's tone left no doubt that he didn't believe Edwards. "Might it not be that your visits were in fact made as a direct result of possessing that knowledge?"

"That's ridiculous! I went as a relative and a friend."

"Ah, yes. Yesterday, you made it quite clear to my men that you looked down on the Hardwickes as being your social inferiors. The late Mrs Hardwicke was even described as coming from 'trade'. Under the circumstances, it's a bit surprising that you chose to develop your association."

For the third time, there was silence from Edwards.

"Another thing, Mr Edwards. Colonel Hardwicke tells us that on your visits you went out of your way to agree with absolutely everything he said. 'Obsequious' was one of the nicer adjectives he used. Yet when my men interviewed you yesterday, you presented an alternative character – your true one, I suspect. And, perhaps pertinently, you said that the colonel 'often talked rubbish'. You can understand why people might think you were ingratiating yourself with him, for some ulterior purpose."

"I didn't always agree with him. I'm sure I said several times he was wrong on some point."

"Did you really? I wonder if the other guests at Hardwicke's table would recall any such incident. You can be sure we will ask them," said Bryce pointedly.

"When and how did you hear about the death of Mrs Beth Hardwicke?"

"I can't say exactly. Last Wednesday, I think. Lady Ainscough telephoned me to inform me of her mother's passing. I'd met her at Mistram once before, so she knew I was a relation. She gave me the funeral details, and invited me to the wake."

"Last Wednesday, yes. Interesting.

"A few minutes ago, you clearly told us that you have never possessed any strychnine. Yet it seems that last Thursday morning you went along to Mr Mills' shop not far from here, and bought a quantity of it. Hardly so long ago that you might have forgotten."

Edwards' face, already pale under Bryce's questions, now turned white and he began to breathe very fast. Nobody else moved.

"Do you deny that?" asked Bryce.

"Yes. No – you're confusing me."

"No, Mr Edwards, you're confusing yourself. The chemist can identify you. And your vicar denies that there are any rats in his church.

"I'll tell you what I think. You were ordained into the Church, but were appointed to a curacy in an area which wasn't to your liking. You found out that the Mistram living was within the gift of Colonel Hardwicke, a distant relative by marriage. You also discovered that the living enjoyed an unusually large endowment income – and it was of course in an area which was far more to your taste than the place to which you had been sent. You decided to get into the colonel's good books, thinking perhaps that you might somehow become rector one day.

"Exactly when you made the decision that you couldn't wait for the incumbent's preferment, retirement, or natural death, I can't say. But when you learned that you would be going to Mrs Hardwicke's funeral, and that your rival would obviously be present, you realised you had an opportunity. So, you obtained some poison. It wasn't difficult to slip it into the rector's coffee, because people were crowded around the table in the parlour.

"I'll go back to my earlier question – what did you do with the bottle?"

Edwards' head was now resting on the table, and he was weeping uncontrollably. All resistance had now left him, and without lifting his head, he muttered:

"I washed it out in the bathroom, went down to the Roding, took the stopper out, and threw it in the river."

"Thank you.

"John Edwards, I charge you with the murder of Simeon Watson, on Tuesday last, at Mistram Manor in the county of Oxfordshire, contrary to Common Law.

"These officers will take you to Oxford later today, and tomorrow you will appear in custody before whichever magistrates' court covers Mistram. I suggest you need a solicitor pretty urgently, although I have to say I don't think either he or counsel will be able to do much for you.

"In fact, being brutally frank, I suggest you start thinking about making your peace with God. In about two months, a judge with a square of black cloth on top of his wig will be saying '… and may the Lord have mercy on your soul'. Bryce stood up.

"But to me you're a cold, calculating, greedy murderer, Edwards. The fact that you are a man of the cloth makes the crime even more heinous, if that were possible. Personally, I don't think your soul, if you have one, deserves any mercy."

The DCI turned away from the curate in disgust, and left the remaining formalities to his men.

****

Haig and Kittow drove back to Oxford. The prisoner, still snivelling intermittently, sat hunched up in the back seat, his handcuffs attached via a chain to a fixed anchoring point in the car.

"That was a classic interview by the guv, Adam. An example to us both. No need for the rubber hoses like they say some coppers used to get confessions in the old days.

"This is the fifth murder case I've seen him handle. In two he actually had some sympathy for the killer – and I agreed with him. But this is the first time I've heard him express loathing – and again I agree with what he said. Watson may have been a Jekyll and Hyde character, but Edwards is my idea of evil."

****

Bryce returned to his office. He already had a number of calls to make, but on reaching his desk he found a note asking him to contact the police laboratory. Moving this call to the top of his list, he rang Hendon.

He received the information that strychnine

had been confirmed in the residue of one of the coffee cups submitted for analysis. The fingerprints on that cup included those of the deceased. A formal report was promised shortly. Thanking the scientist, Bryce asked him to retain the cup, or at least any other prints on it, for the time being. He didn't expect to find that Edwards hand touched it, and it didn't really matter anyway, but it was always worth a check.

Next, he telephoned Superintendent Denton to confirm the arrest, and to ask him to inform his Chief Constable.

His report to the Assistant Commissioner came next, followed by his fourth and last strictly business call – to Travis McKay. He informed McKay of the arrest, and asked him to pass the information on to the coroner, as there was no longer any reason to delay the inquest.

Finally, he called the Manor. Colonel Hardwicke, who was sitting in his study, picked up the telephone himself.

"I just wanted to confirm that Edwards has admitted the murder of Mr Watson," said Bryce. "We have eye-witness evidence of his purchase of the strychnine, so it's now watertight.

"I charged him this morning, and he's on his way to Oxford as we speak. He'll appear before a magistrate tomorrow.

"I've told the coroner that there's no reason to delay the inquest, so I guess that will be held early next week. Whether the coroner will call witnesses, I can't say.

"When this gets to the Assizes, goodness knows how Edwards' counsel will play it. Miles and Angie can give you their professional views. All I'd say is, although Edwards admitted the murder in front of three witnesses, a guilty plea to a capital charge would be most unusual. I suspect his counsel will go for insanity. Given the degree of planning beforehand, and his disposal of the remaining evidence after, I don't give him much chance of success. Having said that, it's always hard to describe anyone who behaves like Edwards as completely sane.

"This is in the public domain now, colonel, so you can take the gags off your family. And – it's up to you of course – you might care to let the other suspects know."

"Damned good job, Bryce," said the colonel, relief evident in his voice despite the crackle on the line. "I'm sure the Chief Constable will be writing a letter of commendation to the Commissioner, but I'll speak to him to ensure that he does.

"Now, I've asked Miles and Angie to negotiate with you and your good lady about a long weekend here. It will be something for me to look forward to. So please don't be reluctant!"

****

BOOKS BY THIS AUTHOR

The Bedroom Window Murder

Detective Chief Inspector Bryce is assigned to a murder case where the county police force has requested the Yard's help.

A local notable, Sir Francis Sherwood, has been found by an open window in his bedroom, shot dead. A rifle, its serial number filed off, is found in the grounds.

The first problem for the Yard men is that nobody with even a mild dislike of Sherwood can be found. But before that difficulty can be solved, others arise...

The Courthouse Murder

In July 1949, an unpopular and deeply unpleasant man is stabbed to death in the courthouse of an English city. As the murder has been committed in a room to which the general public doesn't have access, it seems probable that the culprit is someone involved with the business of the courts.

Suspects include a number of lawyers, police officers, and magistrates.

For various reasons, the local Chief Constable decides to ask Scotland Yard to investigate the murder.

Chief Inspector Philip Bryce and Sergeant Alex Haig are assigned to the case.

The Felixstowe Murder

In August 1949, Detective Chief Inspector Philip Bryce and his new bride Veronica are holidaying in the East Anglian resort of Felixstowe.

During afternoon tea in the Palm Court of their hotel, a man dies at a nearby table.

Reluctant to get directly involved, Bryce nevertheless agrees to help the inexperienced local police inspector – turning his honeymoon into a 'busman's holiday'.

Multiples Of Murder

Three cases for DCI Philip Bryce:

Death in an Office Kitchen
Death in the Public Baths
Death on a London Bus

The first two are set in 1949. The third is a 'prequel', going back to 1946, when Bryce – having returned to the police after army service – was still a Detective Inspector, based in Whitechapel rather than Scotland Yard.

Printed in Great Britain
by Amazon